Kilgannon

They hanged Marshal John Kilgannon's brother in the Hollow and threatened to do the same to his wife unless he released the outlaw 'Dynamite' Ring Burgoyne from the town jail. But the prisoner had gone – taken away for trial by Federal Marshal Brent Blake – and now Kilgannon had a problem.

With his wife in danger and his job under threat from crooked councillor Abraham Levin, Kilgannon was forced to snatch the prisoner. But in that bloody encounter a lawman was blinded by Kilgannon's bullet. And to add to his problems, Burgoyne and his gang are planning a train robbery.

With only his gunfighting skills and the help of old-timer Salty Wood, Kilgannon must face a hail of bullets . . . and come out still standing.

Kilgannon

WILL KEEN

A Black Horse Western

ROBERT HALE · LONDON

ISBN 0 7090 7804 8

Robert Hale Limited
Clerkenwell House
Clerkenwell Green
London EC1R 0HT

Typeset by
Derek Doyle & Associates, Shaw Heath.
Printed and bound in Great Britain by
Antony Rowe Limited, Wiltshire

CHAPTER ONE

They came for John Kilgannon before dawn when the heavy summer rain beating on the tin roof was an insistent drumming that blotted out all other sounds, the only light the occasional sizzling flash of blue-white lightning. It was in the blackness that was the total absence of light after one fierce flash that they kicked the door in, the splintering crash heard even above the incessant downpour. Then they were all over him, the men crowding into the small room overpowering him even as, swearing and half asleep, he flung himself sideways in a tangle of bedclothes to fumble on the sawn-down barrel that was his bedside table for the gunbelt with its worn Colt .45.

The warm rain streaming from their slickers soaked him as they dragged him from his blankets. He could smell the clean night air, acrid sweat, the stink of liquor on hot breath soured by nervous excitement. When he swung a fist wildly at an indistinct face a pistol barrel scythed out of the darkness behind him and sudden agony drove him down on one knee with his head hanging in a blood-red haze.

With their hard hands under his arms they dragged him out, his bare feet trailing. He groaned, gritted his teeth, blood from his ripped scalp dripping on the wet earth floor of his living-room. There they threw his clothes at him and waited in impatient silence while he dressed, then pushed him out into the rain. Other men were in the deeply rutted road; he counted six of them, mounted, looking back uneasily towards Straw's main street. Misshapen Stetsons sagged, pouring water onto shiny slickers. Their stoic horses were steaming and miserable.

The men who had dragged him from the rough cabin that had been his marital home now bundled him onto his bay mare, standing saddled and ready. He slumped forward as his head spun, grabbed for the horn as sickness welled in his throat. The waiting men had already wheeled their mounts. Those behind him now crowded close. A quirt rose and fell. His horse squealed, and shot forward.

And still not a word had been spoken.

Closely bunched, hooves splashing through pools of standing water, they streamed clattering away from the house and swung up the steep slope that cut through the dripping Ponderosa pines marking the edge of town. Kilgannon was hemmed in, swaying in the saddle. After half a mile, the last solitary dwelling behind them, they left the scant shelter of the trees and out on the open flat land the rain was caught by the gusting wind and driven hard into their faces. Someone cursed. Another man laughed harshly.

The wind eased. They pushed onward at a fierce pace. Kilgannon had no time to think. The sickness passed, the effects of the savage blow to the head receded to a dull ache and, conscious of the drying blood on his neck, he struggled to gather his thoughts. He was bewildered, swamped by a deluge of unanswerable questions. He had no idea who these silent men were, or where they were taking him. Or why. Or what he had done to provoke them.

But he was by nature phlegmatic. The hectic pace could not be maintained and, as the riders surrounding him pulled their horses back to a steady canter, his strength began to return, his head cleared. Common sense told him that, if he was to be murdered, they would have shot him where he slept rather than ride needlessly through the fierce summer storm to a place of execution. They were keeping him alive for a reason. When that reason became clear, his unvoiced questions would be answered.

After a while the beating rain slackened, then stopped. Overhead the dark, wind-driven clouds shredded, thinned. Light from the distant dawn was a thin blaze of light spanning the horizon under leaden skies massing to the east. Ahead of the silent riders the timber once again thickened on both sides of the rough road, and now Kilgannon heard one of the men at the head of the party speak gruffly, saw an arm raised, chopped down in silent command.

The hollow, Kilgannon realized: that's where they're taking me. A couple of miles from town, it was a wild expanse of coarse prairie grass split by bald patches and hummocks and dotted with trees stunted by weather that was marked by extremes. In a Montana winter the place was either windswept, flooded or iced over; on a good summer's day it was as hot as Hades, and a place to avoid.

If I was taking a man to his death, he thought, I could choose no place more inhospitable – and suddenly he was seized by an irrational fear that demolished the logic of his earlier thoughts and sent an icy shiver down his spine.

When he regained control of himself the lead riders were already turning off the road, urging their horses through the trees and down the steep bank of brambles and weeds and pulling the other men after them onto the expanse of the hollow to jolt across bumpy ground and splash through pools of standing water to where a battered old Concord stood alongside a tall, skeletal live oak that reared stark and black against eerie skies.

And in his horror Kilgannon saw that beneath a gnarled and crooked bough whose tip had long ago been raggedly severed by a jagged fork of summer lightning a limp figure was a lifeless weight dangling at the end of a rope, twisting lazily until all slack was taken up then spinning just as slowly in the opposite direction . . . again, and again. . . .

They've hanged a man, he thought, and I was wrong after all because now they'll hang me. And without thought he kicked hard with his heels and swung the startled bay mare sideways into the slickered man on his right and the two horses came hard together with a wet slapping sound and the man grunted a curse and hung on to the horn and, as he did so, Kilgannon's world once again exploded in lightning that was an unbearable pressure contained within his skull and his muscles turned to water and he slumped forward as a searing flash of dazzling light gave way to blackness.

He awoke to a singing in his head, felt the stickiness of sweat and the terrible sickness of a desert wanderer light-headed with the stupefying heat and knew the humming was a tormenting cloud of mosquitoes that would slowly drive him mad. He grunted, flapped his arms. Someone laughed, and when he opened his eyes it was to warm and gentle rain and the horror of a crooked bough from which a black shape dangled. He was still in the saddle. He had been unconscious for mere seconds and had woken to a nightmare.

He was flanked by two riders, one of whom had administered the second fierce pistol-whipping. Each man held one of his arms, and now they jerked him cruelly erect in the saddle. Kilgannon felt the earth sway dizzily beneath him. Acrid bile welled, and he hung his head and retched. When he looked up again, a big man – he who at the head of the bunch had lifted his arm to point the way – had moved his horse under the live oak's gnarled limb. As Kilgannon watched, he stood high in his stirrups. Water sprayed from his slicker as he brushed it aside and reached up with one gloved hand. Clawed fingers grabbed a tangle of lank wet hair. He wrenched back the hanged man's head, and in an ashen face the dead eyes rolled and their glistening whites gazed sightlessly at the luminous dawn skies.

'Recognize him, Kilgannon?'

The first words spoken since he had been dragged from his bed, a question and statement rolled into one, three words that in their ringing mockery told him everything and nothing and in their emptiness filled him with agony and despair.

'Yes. I recognize him.' He almost choked on the words, his eyes fixed on the upturned, swollen white face, the strong hand twisting the head back against the pressure of the hangman's knot.

'His name?'

'Kilgannon.'

The big man's grin was mocking. 'Hell, and here's me thinking you were Kilgannon.'

'I have a brother. His name is Daniel.'

'No, Kilgannon. You had a brother. Now all you've got is this, this stinking hunk of cold, dead meat.'

'Damn you,' Kilgannon said fiercely. 'Damn you to hell and back. I don't know you, I'm damned sure you don't know Daniel – so why this murder?'

'To drive home an important point: we never, ever, make idle threats.' The big man released Daniel Kilgannon's head, settled his bulk back in the saddle, let the hanging corpse's stiffening leg's gently nudge, nudge his shoulder as he waited for Kilgannon's reaction.

'All right,' Kilgannon said, and his unsteady voice dripped scorn. 'My brother's been brought to the hollow and hanged; you've done what you set out to do and convinced me you mean business – so if there's any point to this, now comes the threat.'

'Twenty-four hours from now,' the big man said,

'at the next cold dawn, there'll be a slender, real purty body hanging alongside your brother. I guess I don't need to tell you that woman's name – and you know my big turnip watch is already ticking.'

As an ice-cold hand clutched at his heart and a vision of his beautiful, estranged wife flashed before his eyes, John Kilgannon said, 'For God's sake, what do you want from me?'

'We want you to do something for us, Kilgannon – or, to put it another way, we want you to right a wrong, to undo something that's already been done.'

And, for John Kilgannon, everything was suddenly crystal clear.

CHAPTER TWO

Five miles away, Amy Kilgannon was watching the gaunt, bearded man who, with his fellow outlaws, had burst into Daniel Kilgannon's elegant ranch-house in the cold wet hours before dawn. After a short, bloody struggle, the others had bundled Kilgannon out into the rain-swept darkness and her heart had quaked to the thunder of hoofbeats receding into the distance. This man had been left behind and, without putting the notion to the test, Amy guessed she was a prisoner.

The outlaw was sprawled in Daniel Kilgannon's leather chair, drinking Kilgannon's whiskey, his scuffed leather holster pulled around from his right hip so the gleaming pistol it contained rested in his groin. Ready for action, if she made a break for it, Amy thought. And grimaced.

'Somethin' botherin' you?'

'Yes, you're bothering me. Why don't you go? There's nothing I can do to stop whatever it is that's happening.'

'Ain't nothin' happenin'.'

'Then where have they taken Daniel?'

The man shrugged, tilted the whiskey bottle to his lips, drank deeply. He took the bottle away, belched, and Amy shuddered.

'You don't know? Or won't tell?'

'Lady, I just don't care.'

With a very unladylike snort of exasperation, Amy pushed herself off the settee and paced restlessly, arms folded.

She had walked out on John Kilgannon three weeks ago, and moved in with his brother. It was a move of convenience: she was desperate and had nowhere to go, Daniel had a spare room; she lived in his house but was not his woman. She was aware that few people saw it that way, and she knew that this lean scoundrel was leering at her because he had heard the gossip. The irony was that she had left John Kilgannon after six months of marriage because she abhorred the latent violence of his life: the strong man who had swept a naïve girl from back East off her feet had a job that was romantic, but dirty and dangerous. She had rebelled – and now this had happened. This. Whatever it was.

And not for the first time in the past twenty-one days, she found herself speculating on just what it was Daniel Kilgannon did for a living; what he did to earn money, for one need only take a swift glance at this house and its surroundings to know that he had plenty.

But wealth on its own could never be enough, and that was the second ironic twist of fate: this was the morning Amy had intended to tell Daniel that she was returning home, to a house far less grandiose than this but one that for the past half year she had shared with the man she loved. And she did love John Kilgannon. Six months of marriage could never be reduced to insignificance by an absence of just three weeks; had, in fact, begun to hold more precious memories as each day passed, until the unbearable pain of separation told Amy just how foolish, how immature she had been.

She had left John Kilgannon for reasons that, with hindsight, clearly demonstrated her immaturity, and now . . . now, perhaps, it was too late to put things right.

She caught the lean outlaw looking at her, and she pushed her long, corn-coloured hair back off her face then turned away from him to brush away a tear. Warm sunlight was now flooding through the window and across the polished flooring and scattering of expensive rugs. Beyond the gently sloping meadow she could see the faint smudge of distant Ponderosa pines that marked the outskirts of Straw, a thin plume of smoke rising in the still morning air. John Kilgannon's small house – her house – was hidden by those trees. It was likely that he had lit a fire in the stone grate before heading off to work; that the smoke she could see rose from the stone chimney he had built with his own hands. . . .

So near, yet so very far away.

No words had been spoken by Daniel's abductors, but at one point in the violent struggle Amy thought she'd heard him call out to one of them by name. Did that make his situation better, or worse?

And what about her situation?

Why was she being held?

Would Daniel come back, or was the violence of his taking a portent signifying that much worse was to come?

And it was as those thoughts began to crumble her resolve and brought the first genuine pangs of fear that Amy heard the first swelling rumble of distant hooves.

The outlaws were returning.

She swung around to be met by the mocking gaze of her captor, and suddenly frustration boiled to the surface.

'I'm going,' she cried, and ran for the door.

Moving fast for a big man, he cut her off. One massive hand reached for her shoulder. She twisted away, again lunged for the door. His grin was yellow-toothed, and savage. Almost casually, he swung with a hooked arm and hit her with the side of his clenched fist. The massive blow caught her on the cheekbone, snapped her head back. She reeled, tripped on a loose rug, fell heavily on her back.

She was up on her elbows, shaking her head, when the door burst open.

CHAPTER THREE

The strong heat of the morning sun was lifting mois-
ture from the dark Ponderosa pines as Kilgannon
rode down the hill towards town, forming a soft white
mist that trailed like threads of gossamer from the
high, drooping branches. But the acrid smell stinging his nostrils and spooking the big bay mare told a
mind already deep in shock that something was badly
wrong, and when he emerged from the trees the
sight that met his eyes brought added tension and a
harsh curse to his lips.

The mist drifting away from the trees floated high
to merge with the plume of smoke that rose from
blackened ruins. Of the simple shack into which
Kilgannon had taken his young bride, nothing was
left but the sturdy stone column that had been its
chimney, beneath that a confusion of charred timber
and white ash at whose heart the fire that had
destroyed his home still glowed an angry red.

Now, with hindsight, he could recall that the six
men who had escorted him to the hollow had been
reduced to four when he recovered from the second
pistol-whipping: two had supported him by the arms,

16

a third man with a rifle had stayed back in the shadows while the big man abused Daniel Kilgannon's corpse and said his piece.

In John Kilgannon's fleeting moments of unconsciousness, the other two must have slipped away, ridden back to town and put his house to the torch. They had done it when the rain had eased, and the gentle breeze that dried the ground was sufficient to fan the blaze. And he knew it was an act intended to underline what he had been told: he would comply with their impossible request, or no aspect of his life would be safe from the marauders who had murdered his brother.

More than that, it had for the moment left him naked and defenceless: he had the clothes he stood up in; his six-gun had been by his bed, his rifle and shotgun in their rack.

Head pounding, he dismounted, hitched the bay to the picket fence fronting his yard, and did a quick search. It was time wasted. Nothing had escaped the fierce blaze. All that remained of his weapons were dulled barrels that had been twisted grotesquely by the intense heat.

And then, in a crevice alongside the chimney where a stone had split in the heat and fallen to lodge against an upturned iron cooking pot, he found the amber necklace Amy had left behind when she moved out. Smoke blackened but undamaged, the fine metal thread still linking its stones, it shone with an inner light as he rubbed it on his sleeve and, more than anything else, that simple item of jewellery that had belonged to her grandmother drove home like the thrust of a sharp knife the extent of his loss. For this was not his home, it was their home – and now it was gone, and perhaps with it his dreams of one day, quite soon, taking up where he and Amy had left off.

Kilgannon tucked the amber necklace in the right hand pocket of his denim pants. Then he climbed aboard the bay, and began the short ride into town.

He was stopped several times, first by his nearest neighbour who told him Deputy Marshal Chad Reagan had ridden up from town when the blaze was reported, had noticed Kilgannon's bay was missing and, assuming he was away somewhere and safe, had left the fire to burn out. Not a lot he could do anyway, the neighbour remarked; Straw was too small a town to boast modern facilities like a fire appliance, and a bucket chain from the nearest water to Kilgannon's place would have used up the entire population and still fallen way short.

On the outskirts of town, gunsmith and town councillor Jim Pike was standing tall and aproned outside his shop and pulled him over long enough to commiserate, and Kilgannon thanked him then mentioned that he'd be needing a new pistol and rifle. Across the street the Phoenix Saloon was closed, no sign of Salty Wood, and Kilgannon's next stop was at the general store where he placed a clothing order with proprietor Tom Morgan and arranged to pick up the packages later that day.

Then he again crossed the road, tied the bay to the hitch rail, and went into the jail.

Behind the desk, sprawled in Kilgannon's swivel chair, was the leader of Straw's town council, Abraham Levin. His face was florid, his black string tie loosened, the ends dangling on the crisp white shirt that was strained so tight it would pop some buttons if he took a deep breath. His shrewd, steely-blue eyes watched Kilgannon as he flipped his hat onto a hook and grabbed a chair to sit down on the wrong side of his own desk. Levin had a cigar in his thick fingers and, as he twiddled it restlessly, Kilgannon got the feeling he was a troubled man.

'They tell me you're in trouble,' Levin said.

'News travels real fast, when it's bad.'

Levin's eyes were like steel probes. 'You anything for me, anything to tell me I don't already know?'

Kilgannon said, 'You heard about the fire. I heard Reagan was out at my place, he figured it was out of control and rode away.' He shrugged. 'You need anything else, ask him, he knows more than me.'

'Because, fortuitously, you happened to be some-place else.'

Kilgannon let that one stand.

'And again,' Levin said, 'you've got nothing to tell me?'

'My house burned down,' Kilgannon said, and met the big councillor's hard stare. 'What I stand up in is everything I own.'

Levin took a deep breath, heaved himself out of the chair.

'You need anything, let me know,' he said curtly. 'Your job's on a knife edge, Kilgannon. We don't want your duties further affected by brooding on

19

what's in the past.'

The door slammed, and he was gone.

Dust motes floated in the early sunlight shafting through the window. Kilgannon crossed to the stove, poured a cup of coffee, took a quick drink of the lukewarm brew and grimaced with distaste.

Abraham Levin was crooked. There was no way Kilgannon could prove it – yet – but the leader of the town council was as twisted as a parched mesquite branch and had too much money stashed away for the owner of a humble drug store. There'd been talk of ripping off reservation Indians, of stolen horses sold to the army, of bank foreclosures on struggling ranches in which men paid by Levin had been vicious enforcers.

Never any proof.

But Abraham Levin wanted John Kilgannon out of office, and so to the already ticklish dilemma which Kilgannon faced had been added one more painful complication: Levin smelled a rat, and that was before Kilgannon had reached a decision, before he had committed himself one way or the other.

Ah, well. . . .

He sighed, again tasted the coffee, again pulled a face. Chad Reagan would be in shortly. And, like it or not, that decision must be made.

He put down the cup, sat down behind his desk, slid open a drawer and pinned the gleaming tin badge to his vest and was ready to resume his duties as John Kilgannon, Marshal of Straw, Montana.

It was fully half an hour before it occurred to

Kilgannon that he should have checked on his prisoner. In that time his senses had left him and he
supposed that, to anyone passing by and seeing him
slumped in his chair with eyes staring sightlessly, he
must have looked like a man locked deep in the
coma that precedes death. Which, understandably,
was the way he felt, for it's not every day that a man
is dragged savagely from a peaceful sleep and in the
space of a single hour gazes in horror at his brother's
slack body hanging from a gaunt live oak, and sees
his own home burned to the ground.

Coming as they did on top of the recent stunning
shock of Amy's desertion, these latest body blows
were crippling. He had sipped his coffee, automatically pinned on the badge and, as he sagged back in
his swivel chair, it was as if all the breath had been
driven from his body. Abraham Levin was forgotten.
Stark images flashed before his eyes; memories
evoked such sadness that his mind became numbed;
time stood still, yet dragged on for an eternity that
was pure agony. And now, limp and drained of
emotion, it was only with considerable effort that he
stirred, absently moved the cup of now cold coffee,
and kicked his sluggish brain into some kind of
action.

Immediately, his awakened mind was assailed by
the seriousness of his situation.

The outlaw, Ring Burgoyne, was his prisoner. The
clock on the wall was relentlessly marking the passing
of time. And in the time that was fast running out,
Kilgannon knew he must make a decision.

Listening, Kilgannon heard no sound from the

cells at the rear of the building. Well, Chad Reagan would have served Burgoyne his breakfast and, locked in an eight-by-six strap steel cell, it was reasonable to assume the prisoner had eaten well then flopped on his cot and either smoked cigarette after cigarette or gone back to sleep.

But where was Reagan? A wrangler who'd grown tired of being thrown by broncs from dawn till dusk, he was new, raw, keen on the job and in the couple of months since he'd pinned on the badge he'd proved competent, and reliable. Which made his absence unusual.

Straw's townsfolk went early to work, and there was already a buzz of activity. People on foot were crossing the street in ungainly haste to avoid Stetsoned cowboys on frisky horses and heavy wagons pulled by steaming mule teams, and the air was filled with oaths, deep-voiced greetings, the shrill cries of children skipping to the nearby school and the yapping of the town's stray dogs.

And Reagan, Kilgannon realized, would be in his usual place for this time of day: across the street at the café, watching the jail from his seat in the window while eating a breakfast cooked by his fiancée, Nellie Wynne.

As if at a signal, the big deputy emerged from the café even as Kilgannon reluctantly left his swivel chair and crossed to look out of the window. He saw the big man step down off the opposite sidewalk and, as he dodged his way across the busy street, Kilgannon returned to his desk and tried to look busy.

'Where the hell have you been?' he said gruffly, as the door swung open.

Reagan blinked. 'What happened, you roll out the wrong side of the bed this . . .' – and then he checked. 'Hey,' he said quietly, 'I apologize, John, that was a slip. I heard what happened. I guess as of today you haven't got a bed of any kind to get out of.' He flipped his Stetson onto a wall peg, cocked an eyebrow, his broad features concerned. 'Any idea who burned down your house, and why?'

'Yes, and yes – but leave that for the present,' Kilgannon said, and he sat back and put down his pen. 'What about Burgoyne?'

'All settled,' Reagan said.

'Yeah, seems that way. He's mighty quiet. Too quiet. Maybe we should give the man some exercise.'

Reagan swung around. 'Quiet?' He shook his head. 'No, what I mean is it's wrapped up, Burgoyne's gone, he's out of our hair.'

Kilgannon went cold. His scalp prickled.

'Blake, that federal marshal, he rode in early,' Reagan said.

'Who?'

'Brent Blake.'

'We've never met, don't know him by sight or sound,' Kilgannon said.

'Showed his badge, had a letter authorizing the release of the prisoner into his custody. He took his breakfast at Nellie's, rode out again an hour later with Burgoyne's ankles lashed, his horse on a lead rope.' Reagan hesitated, clearly wondering what was wrong. 'Blake told me the trial's set for next week.

23

Hell, Burgoyne rode into town, murdered that cowpoke for no damn reason, and now he'll hang – that's what you want, isn't it?'

'Sure. But what if he's not alone? He was in town, killed a man – but where did he come from?' Kilgannon forced the words through stiff lips, let the question hang unanswered as the deputy waited for elaboration. Then the swivel chair rocked dangerously as he abruptly thrust his way to his feet. Reagan was watching him oddly. Kilgannon forced a weak grin. 'I didn't get much sleep, Chad, I guess I'm a day behind in my thinking.'

'That's understandable.' Kilgannon knew the brief explanation bore the ring of truth as the big deputy nodded, relieved, his gaze drifting towards the coffee pot even as he loosened his belt to make room for the breakfast he'd just stowed away.

'Listen, feller,' Kilgannon said, 'you stay here, mind the store while I wander up the street. I'll breathe some of that good clean air, clear my head, spend an hour chewing the fat with Salty.'

He clapped the big man on the shoulder, made some throwaway comment that was lost in the renewed turmoil of his emotions before he reached the door. Then he was out on the plankwalk tasting that fresh air he'd mentioned – already thickly larded with the hot, swirling dust of another day – his boots thudding on the timber as he made his way up the street.

He'd gone thirty yards when a thought hit him and he turned back. He knew his actions in the next hour or so would be determined by the decision he must make, and if he wanted to leave town without advertising the fact, the hitch rail in front of his office was no place to start. He untied the bay, crossed the street to Joe Dyson's livery barn – which had a convenient rear door opening onto the alley running parallel to the main street – and in no time at all had arranged with the hostler to have his horse cared for, but ready for instant departure.

Then he again walked back across the street, his lips for a moment twitching with a wry smile at the thought that he seemed to have been doing little else ever since he rode into town.

Most mornings at this time he would leave Chad lazily holding the fort and call in at Conny McPolin's estimable boarding establishment for a friendly chat over yet more coffee. Straw's dark-haired, slender hotel owner was a long-time friend of Kilgannon, had quickly taken to Amy when she'd become Kilgannon's wife but had been paper-tearing furious when she'd walked out on the marshal.

Today, Kilgannon was aware that he would need a bed for the night, but was in no mood for small talk. He glanced once at the hotel's open door, then walked quickly by and on to the Phoenix for some serious talk with the man who had for years been a legend in the town of Straw.

Old Salty Wood was a prospector and trapper who'd grown weary of both tough ways of making a livelihood, ridden down on his mule from the high hills of northern Montana and bought Straw's rundown saloon with fine yellow gold dust poured from a soft leather pouch onto the rough timber bar. He had created a new life for himself – hence the saloon's name – but had forsaken neither his roots nor his image. He wore greasy buckskins and a bushy grey beard, kept an ancient muzzle-loading buffalo gun highly visible behind the bar to deter trouble-makers, and if Marshal Kilgannon wanted information on topics ranging from current prices on the New York Stock Exchange to the likelihood of early snow drawing bears down from the hills to forage in Straw's back alleys then he knew exactly who to consult.

On that clear sunny day his sharp blue eyes showed that he could read trouble written all over Kilgannon's face the minute he walked through the doors. By the time the marshal had kicked a trail through the thin sawdust on the way to the bar, foam was sliding down a tall glass of fresh beer, and Salty was watching his approach out of the corner of his eye while gnawing at his drooping moustaches with teeth yellower than the gold he'd once panned.

'I guess I'd better give up any ideas of playing poker for a living,' Kilgannon said, reaching for the glass.

'It's writ all over your face,' Salty said. 'There's something more than a marriage gone south and a burned-down house bothering you – and to put those events into the shade it must be real bad.'

'Bad enough to addle a man's brain,' Kilgannon said. He took a long drink of cold beer, glanced around the empty saloon. 'Can we talk?'

CHAPTER FOUR

Her head was ringing to the sound of approaching hooves, her eyesight blurred, the side of her face a throbbing ache. But Hack and D'Souza were in the room, the noises in her head nothing but the thundering of her pulse as her heart raced. Again she shook her head, fair hair tumbling in disarray; then she rolled over, struggled to her knees, climbed to her feet. The room spun dizzily, settled.

The bearded man who had remained behind to guard Amy had stumbled backwards as the door crashed open. Now his gaze was shifting warily between Amy and the two men who had burst into the room.

Hack's single good eye fastened on the empty whiskey bottle on the floor by the leather chair. His face tightened. He'd watched Amy climb off the floor. Now he looked closer at her face, noted the raised hand, the bruises visible through her thick fair hair that fell forward as she lowered her head and winced. With a shake of his head he turned, swung a booted foot and sent the bottle flying across the room to shatter against the wall.

'You'll have to pardon my friend,' D'Souza said, grinning at Amy, 'but he had a religious upbringing and don't condone violence or hard drinking.'

'But killing's OK,' Amy said, 'so where's Daniel?'

'You think he's dead?'

'After the way you burst in here, dragged him from his bed?' Amy's voice was scornful. 'No, I think you wiped the blood off his face, took him into town and bought him a drink in the Phoenix—'

'Maybe we did just that.'

Hack, his big fist clenched on the man's shirt neck, was hustling the bearded outlaw out of the room. He stumbled into the hall, Hack slammed the door behind him, turned and stood with his back against it. The scar disfiguring his cheek was livid; the dead eye was as white as a fish's belly.

What do they want with me, Amy wondered? The same question she had asked herself all morning – and still it went unanswered because she knew these two men would tell her nothing unless it was to their advantage.

'All right,' she said. Face throbbing, she sat down with her hands folded in her lap, forcing herself to be calm. 'You took Daniel into town. But why would you do that? Why take him at all?'

'He's John Kilgannon's brother. Daniel's ... *persuading* Kilgannon' – the two men exchanged knowing grins – 'that as marshal of Straw he's in a position to do us a small favour.'

'Such as?'

'Well now, you're the marshal's woman, why don't you make a wild guess?'

For a moment Amy was flummoxed. She had been away from Kilgannon for three weeks, so was a little behind with the news. But she did suddenly recall that the big occasion prior to her walkout had been the arrest of Ring Burgoyne, and if this morning's events were connected to that outlaw's imprisonment . . .

'If you think John will be talked into releasing the ruffian who murdered a cowboy in cold blood,' she said, 'then you'd better think again.'

D'Souza winked at Hack.

'You're right, a marshal walking the straight and narrow wouldn't do that,' he said, 'but there may be something hidden in his past your man ain't told you about.'

'What do you mean?' Amy said, her mouth suddenly, unaccountably dry.

'You know he's not from these parts?'

'I . . . we haven't discussed it.'

'Got a southern drawl when you listen close – wouldn't you say?'

'All right, yes, I've noticed that, but it has never come up in conversation.'

'My guess,' D'Souza said, 'is he'd knock you back if you mentioned it, because your man's kinda cagey about the life he once led.'

And now Amy's heart was thudding, and she had to clasp her hands firmly in her lap to disguise their trembling.

'I . . . I don't know what you mean, you're just making those horrible insinuations to frighten me.'

'No, ma'am,' D'Souza said, 'I ain't. If there's

anybody around here should be scared, then I'd say it's Kilgannon. He's been doin' his damnedest to bury a reputation that's as cold and black as a December night. But there's a man right there in Straw got him weighed up a coupla years ago, and that feller also bears Kilgannon one almighty big grudge he aims to settle real soon.'

CHAPTER FIVE

'It was Burgoyne's cronies,' Kilgannon said.

Salty grimaced. 'Didn't take much figuring out: you toss him in the hoosegow, they retaliate by burning down your house.'

'No,' Kilgannon said, then gestured helplessly. 'All right, yes, they did – but before that, there was worse, much worse.' He could hear the break in his voice, and he hesitated, then swallowed and went on, 'Before dawn, six men came riding out of the rain, dragged me from my bed.' His mind again filled with haunting scenes of horror, one hand lifted, his fingers tracing the jagged wounds in his scalp. 'They took me to the hollow, to that dead oak standing by the old Concord. Daniel was there. I suppose they'd done much the same to him, dragged him from his warm bed into the rain. But there was a difference. When they led Daniel down into the hollow, they tied the end of a rope around that big bough then placed the noose around his neck. And they took considerable delight in telling me how they used a quirt to drive the horse out from under him, stood by and watched him kick as he took time dying.'

'Jesus!' Salty breathed softly.

The two men were lost in the dim light of the Phoenix saloon. The window blinds had been down when Kilgannon walked in. When he told Wood he needed to talk, the old saloonist had quickly closed the doors. Now they were both at the bar, Kilgannon on a stool, Salty Wood around the business side with a whiskey bottle close to his hand.

In the heavy silence Salty said, 'That would be Ring Burgoyne's doing. You've been decent enough to allow that scar-faced feller with the dead eye in to see him, and it don't take a genius to figure out what Burgoyne's done, why he'd order the hanging of your brother. He wants out of that cell, right? – and to force your hand he's holding the threat of the noose he used on Daniel over someone's head?'

'Amy.'

'He's got her?'

'So he says.'

Salty nodded, his brow knitted as he chewed his moustache and thought through the story he'd accurately fathomed using nothing but logic and a shrewd knowledge of the kind of man opposing Kilgannon.

'And now the big question,' he said at last. 'What do you do to get out of this fix?' And with a glance at Kilgannon with one sharp blue eye cocked and his bearded face twisted into a fierce grin, he tilted the whiskey bottle over the marshal's glass, poured out a stiff measure – and waited.

Kilgannon ignored the drink.

'The hard answer is, I don't know what to do,' he

said. 'For a moral man there is no right answer. After that cowpoke was murdered, my duty was to pull in Ring Burgoyne and ensure he got to trial. That's been done. But seems he wasn't alone when he rode into the territory. Now Burgoyne and his outlaws want the clock put back, what's been done undone, things put back the way they were. If I buckle under, do what they say, my career's over. But if I leave things as they stand, my wife dies.'

'I thought Burgoyne was still cosy in one of your cells?'

Kilgannon shook his head. 'He was picked up this morning by a feller called Blake, a federal marshal, round about the time my house went up in flames.'

'Which complicates matters.'

'Right. If I decide to throw in my badge, save Amy, it's no longer simply a matter of turning the key in a lock and looking the other way. I've got to ride out in a hurry, take him from another officer of the law – and I can't see that happening without actual physical violence.'

And now Kilgannon did pick up the glass. With one quick jerk of the wrist he tossed back the shot of whiskey, let the fiery spirit burn his throat and for an instant take his mind off the insoluble problem that was threatening to tear him apart. Then he gasped, met the clear gaze of the watching old-timer – and shrugged helplessly.

'Like you, those fellers who hanged my brother believe Ring Burgoyne's still in my jail. They've given me until sunset to deliver him to them, unharmed. If I don't, I have no doubt they'll put a noose around

Amy's neck and hang her from that same tree in the hollow.'

He put the empty glass down on the bar with a hollow thud.

'So the question you threw at me is back with you, old friend. How do I retain my integrity as a lawman, yet at the same time save a young woman – who also happens to be my wife – from a horrible death?'

And as if he had abandoned any hope of resolving the crisis, Kilgannon unpinned the shiny tin marshal's badge, glanced at it ruefully and dropped into his pants' pocket alongside Amy's amber necklace.

For a few moments both men stood on opposite sides of the timber bar, lost in thought. Kilgannon was vaguely aware of the myriad sounds of Straw's busy main street reaching them as a low murmur muted by the heavy window blinds and the closed door, but his mind was numb and what thoughts he could muster had a habit of going round in such a tightly closed circle that he felt dizzy, his breathing tight and strained.

The whiskey had warmed his throat, but left his shocked emotions as cold as a Montana winter. He had posed a question, but could see no possible answer. Already suffering from intense feelings of guilt because, as town marshal, he was automatically accepting responsibility for his brother's death, he was also aware that he had selfishly placed on Salty Wood's shoulders the burden of a responsibility that was not his to bear. Kilgannon was town marshal, the frightening dilemma dumped in his lap was his to resolve – yet he felt powerless, a desperate poker player overwhelmed by the cruel actions of men outside the law who held all the high cards. . . .

'On your own,' Salty Wood said, cutting through his thoughts, 'you're faced with an impossible decision. You know that, you've asked for my opinion, but you're talking to the wrong man.'

'Who else?' Kilgannon said bitterly.

'The federal man, Blake.'

'I know his reputation. He's hard as nails, a dedicated lawman who looks at a bleak world in pure black and white.'

'Talk to him.'

'And ask him to release Ring Burgoyne? He'll think I've gone crazy.'

Wood's blue eyes were glinting with a devilish light. 'When you're faced by a crazy situation, think crazy. You're a strong man, John, fazed by something came out of the blue that hit you like a runaway steer. Your brother's been strung up, he's still out there now when you want him decently buried. At times like this, logical thinking goes out the window. I remember one time, up in the mountains with my leg broke and snow so thick it was halfway up the trees—'

'Yeah,' Kilgannon said, 'I remember you telling me about that one.'

'What I did then was more than crazy, but it worked.'

'I know it did, and I know you're right. Asking Brent Blake to turn a prisoner loose is so damned loco he might just do it – and when it all boils down, what choice have I got?'

'If he won't do it,' Salty said with a grin, 'tell him he'll be up agin a fiery old trapper keeps an old buffalo gun propped in the corner for use on ornery lawmen.'

'Oh, he'll do it,' Kilgannon said, for the first time that morning feeling the onset of a spontaneous smile. 'Hell, no sane man could be that crazy!'

CHAPTER SIX

As he rode down the rubbish-littered alley behind Joe Dyson's livery barn and so out of Straw without being seen, John Kilgannon estimated that Federal Marshal Brent Blake and his prisoner Burgoyne had the best part of three hours' start on him – and mentally cursed the time he'd wasted.

If he hadn't been so badly and uncharacteristically thrown by what had happened, his own level head and shrewd thinking would have brought him to Salty Wood's possible solution to his problem while he was drinking his first cup of coffee in the office. Instead, he'd slipped into a daze of maudlin self-pity that had knocked him sideways and lost him valuable time he couldn't afford.

The only consolation was that he'd borrowed a gunbelt carrying an old Colt .45 from Salty, his bay mare was rested, watered and fed, and so it was with confidence that Kilgannon gave the eager horse her head as they hit the open country.

He made good speed, his body singing to the exhilaration aroused by springing into action after a morning spent wallowing in gloom. If there was anything to cast a dark shadow over his mood it was that his ride was taking him perilously close to the hollow where the body of his brother still hung beneath the tall oak tree. But Kilgannon knew that the action he was embarking on now should prove decisive. Blake would co-operate, Kilgannon would secure Amy's release, a decent burial for Daniel Kilgannon would follow, and the whole black episode would become no more than a cruel, fading memory.

With those optimistic thoughts to encourage him, he rode on in good heart. Around him the mountains reared tall and timber-cloaked as the big mare sped along a trail that climbed to dizzy heights and swooped into valleys where fast waters roared over glistening black rocks. And always his eyes were skinned, narrowed against the wind and bright sunlight as he peered ahead for any sign of his quarry.

For he knew full well that to come up on a man like Brent Blake at speed and without warning was to invite a volley of shots from a man who, in this situation, would shoot first and asked questions later.

A hard man, so Kilgannon had heard, with set ideas and a mind that, once made up, was as immovable as the Montana rock. And this was the man, he admitted wryly, he was hoping to sweet-talk into releasing a killer.

Nevertheless, despite the difficulties that lay ahead he rode on with hope still high and all his senses alert – and that watchfulness was to pay off. He made one stop, took a long draught of cool water from his canteen, tipped the rest into his hat for the mare to drink while he listened to the woodland silence, then pushed on hard. He kept that up for another five miles until, with the bay down to a cautious trot where the trail dipped between dark pines flanking a tumbling stream, for the second time that day Kilgannon's nose detected the faint smell of wood smoke.

'Easy,' he said softly, and shivered at awakened memories as he patted the mare's slick neck and reined in.

He was hemmed in by trees through which little could be seen other than steep slopes on both sides, patches of bright blue sky above and ahead where the woodland gradually thinned. But mingling with the dark green of the pines Kilgannon's sharp eyes picked up the thin haze of white smoke from the fire, and he knew that, despite his caution, he'd damn near ridden into Blake's temporary camp.

'And that really would have torn it,' he murmured, then touched the mare lightly with his heels and moved her on.

As he moved along the bank above the rushing white waters, Kilgannon began to whistle.

He dug deep and came up with a lively barn dance jig, whistled it tunelessly but loud enough to be heard above the noise of the torrent. He was under no illusions that Blake would be fooled into dropping his guard. A lonely traveller might whistle to keep up his spirits but, to the ever cautious marshal, Kilgannon's whistling would smack of a ruse employed by a dangerous stranger to hold his attention.

But at least he'd be more likely to hold his fire.

The marshal and his prisoner had halted in a glade set back from the trail. Both horses were ground tethered and, when Kilgannon rode in, a tall man with a badge gleaming on his vest was kicking earth over the fire's embers and preparing to move.

Ring Burgoyne was already in the saddle, ankles lashed under the belly of a ragged sorrel, his free hands folded on the horn as he waited.

It was the outlaw who first acknowledged his presence. Even from across the glade, Kilgannon saw the flash of recognition in the glittering black eyes, the quick, sardonic grin.

But Burgoyne said nothing.

At last, Brent Blake looked up.

'Howdy,' Kilgannon called. 'Thought I'd be in time for coffee, but it seems I'm too late.'

The man grunted.

'You're Brent Blake?' Kilgannon said.

And now Blake's manner underwent a change.

'Ride on,' he said, and his voice was as hard as tempered steel.

'We need to talk.'

The federal marshal's eyes were guarded. 'You and me?' He looked Kilgannon up and down, flicked a glance to both sides of the glade and shook his head. 'I don't think so.'

Suddenly Kilgannon was aware of the image he presented to the lawman. Before dawn he had been dragged from his bed into the driving rain, beaten about the head with a six-gun not once but twice; he was tired, unshaven and unwashed – and, too late, he could feel the patch of stiff dried blood on his neck. To Blake, he was a ruffian who had whistled a tune as he rode in out of nowhere. Worse, it was possible he was one of Ring Burgoyne's men creating a diversion, and the federal man was conscious of the menace of the encroaching woods and in a hurry to move to safety.

Kilgannon was a lawman with the appearance of an outlaw – and the badge of office that could have saved him was tucked away in his pants' pocket.

Even as those thoughts crossed Kilgannon's mind, the tall federal lawman had swung into the saddle. He trotted his horse across to the waiting Burgoyne, bent to pick up the dangling lead rope, and began leading the outlaw towards the trail.

'Wait,' Kilgannon said. 'We need to talk about Ring Burgoyne—'

'You know Burgoyne, that's the end of it,' Blake snapped. 'Now get the hell out of my way, feller.'

'No, hold on, I'm from Straw, I'm—'

And then he made his mistake.

As he spoke, his hand was moving quickly and impulsively towards his pocket for the badge that would back up the announcement he was about to make and convince Blake that he came with authority. But a rawhide cord lashed Salty Wood's holster to his right thigh and Blake, out of the corner of his eye, caught the swift stab of Kilgannon's hand towards his pocket. In the circumstances he could come to but one conclusion: Kilgannon was going for his gun.

Blake dropped the reins. He twisted in the saddle,

made a draw so fast that to Kilgannon it was a blur of movement. His six-gun cracked, the muzzle-flash bright in the shadowy glade. Kilgannon, his right hand already reaching into his pocket, felt the wind of the bullet as it whined past his face. A second shot cracked. He flung himself from the saddle, fell on his side with his right hand trapped. A third shot kicked dirt into his face. He rolled, saw the marshal's six-gun following him, saw the grim determination in the lawman's clenched jaw and flat gaze.

With a mighty effort Kilgannon freed his hand. He grabbed for Salty's old six-gun, made a snatched, fumbling draw, cast another swift glance towards the federal lawman and knew he was too late: it was over, finished.

Then Burgoyne moved. He kicked his horse savagely. It squealed, reared high, hooves flailing – and the lead rope was wrenched from Blake's hand, pulling him half out of the saddle.

But he wasn't done. As his startled horse danced sideways he snarled and grabbed for the horn with his left hand. Hanging on by that one hand and his leg awkwardly hooked over the saddle, he again swung his six-gun towards Kilgannon.

Grimly, teeth clenched, Kilgannon lifted his six-gun and fired.

Blake's head jerked. His Stetson flew into the air. Then his body went loose and he was flung backwards out of the saddle.

He hit the hard ground on his shoulders. His left foot was caught in the stirrup. Terrified by now, his horse backed away, stumbled, almost went down, then leaped sideways and broke into a run.

Still fighting to regain his feet, Kilgannon watched in mounting horror.

Blake was dragged for thirty yards, his body bouncing on the ground like a limp sack of grain. Then his foot came free. In the cloud of dust kicked up by the running horse, he rolled, and lay without moving.

The glade became still and silent. Gunsmoke cleared. Dust hung in the dappled sunlight.

Of the outlaw, Ring Burgoyne, there was no sign.

On his feet again, Kilgannon stood for several moments in stunned silence. Warm blood trickled down his neck from the reopened scalp wounds. There was a persistent, nagging ache behind his eyes, and a dull feeling of inevitability that was like a thick black cloud obscuring all hope. It was decision time once again, but this time the decision would be made by a man whose life had changed dramatically and irrevocably. Kilgannon took immense pride in his achievement of becoming a lawman respected by the citizens of Straw, but that respected lawman had committed a crime: he had gunned down another officer, and his actions had allowed an outlaw to escape.

The only bright shaft of light penetrating the black cloud was the knowledge that Burgoyne would find his way back to his cronies, and that proof of his release – as a consequence of Kilgannon's compliance with the outlaws' demands – should be enough to buy Amy her freedom. Should. For Kilgannon was all too well aware that he would be foolish to expect any outlaw to keep his word.

But that was a problem to be faced at another time, in another place. Of more urgent concern was the condition of the man he had gunned down, and it was with a feeling of intense dread that John Kilgannon forced his feet to carry him across the glade to where Brent Blake lay in the dust, a pool of dark blood forming under his head.

From his pocket, Kilgannon took and pinned on the badge that had caused the trouble. Then he dropped to his knees alongside the downed marshal. The man's dark hair was matted with blood, and Kilgannon saw the long, ragged groove where his bullet had sliced through the scalp above the marshal's ear. It was shallow; there were no bone splinters. Gingerly, Kilgannon took hold of Blake's shoulders and rolled him onto his back. Blake's arm flopped limply. His head canted sideways. Holding his breath, Kilgannon placed two fingers on the warm neck – and felt a strong pulse. He closed his eyes, rocked back on his heels, then for an instant cast his eyes towards the heavens and said a silent prayer of thanks.

When he looked down again, Blake's eyes had opened, and he was looking straight at Kilgannon.

Kilgannon swallowed. 'You're going to be OK,' he said. 'A slug grazed your scalp, opened up a shallow wound that knocked you out.'

The marshal winced, half reached up to the wound, let his hand fall. 'Thanks for your help. But the feller who did this – where is he?'

Kneeling as he was alongside the wounded man,

pinned by his direct gaze, the question took
Kilgannon by complete surprise. He could only imagine that Blake was still groggy – yet the man appeared
clear headed, and the question had been voiced
strongly, and without hesitation.

'Didn't you see him?'

'Sure I did,' Blake said.

And now Kilgannon was perplexed.

'Then . . . ?'

'Well, he rode in, took a shot at me – then I guess
you came along and he got rattled and hightailed.
Isn't that what happened?'

Still flummoxed, clutching at any straws tossed his
way, Kilgannon said vaguely, 'Something like that. I
was in the area . . . heard shooting. . . .'

'Good for you. All I know is he was a tall feller on
a bay horse, a ruffian by the looks of him, and he was
shouting something about Ring Burgoyne—' Blake
broke off. 'Goddamn! Tell me, is there a feller here
on an apology for a sorrel, ankles lashed . . . ?'

Feeling foolish, Kilgannon deliberately looked
around the empty glade, shrugged, said, 'Nobody
here, see for yourself—'

'Hell, don't you think I'd do that if my eyes'd
work!' Blake blurted, half rising with the force of his
words. Then he fell back, his face red. 'I can't see, for
Christ's sake,' he said, in a voice hoarse with despair.
'The bullet that sliced across my head hit something,
and it took away my sight!'

45

CHAPTER SEVEN

All the way into town, John Kilgannon was aware of Brent Blake's menacing presence behind him. He knew the federal lawman could not see him, but the menace was there nonetheless because being sightless didn't stop the injured man's mind from working. So, for mile after mile, Kilgannon worried constantly about the time that would surely come when something clicked in the man's brain and he realized Kilgannon was the gunman who had taken away his sight.

They chatted desultorily. Kilgannon revealed that he was Straw's marshal, but didn't say why he had been riding near to that forest glade. Blake apologized for taking Burgoyne without waiting to talk to Kilgannon, giving as a reason that the case was a complex one. But mostly they kept their silence, both men lost in thought, and it was a grim pair that rode out of the setting sun into Straw's main street and so to the surgery of Dr Ebenezer Thom.

There, the news was better – for Blake.

'Temporary,' Thom said, in answer to the inevitable question. 'You'll have your sight back before too long.'

'How long?' Blake said.

Thom shrugged, then touched the federal marshal's shoulder. 'A day, a week ... maybe a month. I can't pin it down but, take my word for it, you'll be as good as new.'

Behind wire-framed glasses his grey eyes, wise and unblinking as an owl's, moved to Kilgannon. Suddenly Kilgannon was uncomfortable, for he knew this man well and sensed that Thom was suspicious.

And for the first time that day Kilgannon began musing uneasily on the wider issues involved in what had happened, and how the day's events – and their consequences – might appear to the citizens of Straw.

'Is it OK to move him?'

'Damn right it is,' Blake growled, and Doc Thom laughed.

'He walked in here, John, so I'm sure he can retrace his steps. If he's got a bed for the night, he'll sleep easy and well.'

'There'll be a room for him at Conny's. We'll walk over there, sort things out – and, Eb, thanks for your help.'

Thom wiped his hands, shook hands with both men, and stepped away from the examination table so Blake could swing his legs down and get to his feet. At once, Kilgannon was at the marshal's side.

Back outside they breathed deeply to get rid of the surgery's antiseptic smells, relishing the cooling air of a summer's evening, basking in the whisper of a gentle breeze and the comforting mumble of conversation drifting to them from Salty Wood's Phoenix

Saloon. Then they moved without awkwardness across the quiet, dusty street to where the lighted windows of Conny McPolin's rooming-house beckoned warmly. Kilgannon had his hand cupping the marshal's elbow, but nobody watching would have been aware that Blake was a sightless man being guided every step of the way.

Moments later Blake was booked in, Conny had warmly taken over from a grateful Kilgannon, and with a promise to look in on him later Kilgannon bade the federal marshal goodnight.

In truth, he was mightily relieved to walk away from the man who held behind his sightless eyes the knowledge that could ruin Kilgannon. According to Ebenezer Thom, that knowledge might come to light in a day, a week or a month – but it would certainly arrive and, when it did, Kilgannon was finished.

He stopped some yards down the street, on the edge of the plank walk, looked out over the silent thoroughfare and took some time to roll a cigarette. As he did so, lit up and blew the first plume of smoke towards the dim orb of the moon rising above the false fronts of Nellie's café and Joe Dyson's livery barn, he knew that the accident of a wild gunshot had bequeathed on him the gift of time. A day, a week, a month – it didn't matter. He had precious time to use, and it had always been his belief that a man was in control of his own destiny. So he would use that time well. Already he had achieved what he had considered the impossible: the temporary release of Ring Burgoyne, for which he was indirectly indebted to Salty Wood. Once Kilgannon knew Amy had been released as promised, then Burgoyne *must* be recaptured. Only by putting the outlaw back behind bars could Kilgannon begin to make recompense for his lawless actions. And, he knew, it would be an uphill struggle.

He flicked the cigarette, sent it sparking into the dust. Across the street, the lamp in a building between the café and livery barn was extinguished. Then a door opened, and a man in a dark suit stepped out onto the plank walk. In the wan street lighting his teeth flashed white as he smiled fleetingly and called across to Kilgannon.

'Got a minute, John?'

Kilgannon stepped down, made his way across and shook Courtney Flynn's hand. The lawyer was tall, dark-moustached. He was clever, affable, and an old friend, but the smile had been quickly switched off and his eyes were guarded. He touched Kilgannon's sleeve, moved him back into the deeper shadows close to the door of his office.

'After what happened to Daniel I guess this is a bad time to talk. . . .' He waited, saw Kilgannon's noncommittal shrug, nodded quickly and went on, 'But because of what happened – and I'm not talking only about today – there are certain things you should know as fact, others you should be aware of as possibilities.'

'That's lawyer talk, Courtney, and I don't like it,' Kilgannon said, and without bidding his thoughts flashed back to the suspicion he thought he had seen in the eyes of Ebenezer Thom.

'Yeah,' Flynn said, 'and I'm wearing my professional hat because I don't like some of what I've got to say.'

'So why don't we both back off, then talk over coffee in my office?'

'No.' Flynn shook his head. 'Chad Reagan's on duty. This is not for a deputy's ears.'

Kilgannon sighed. 'I'm tired, Courtney, get on with it.'

In the shadows, the lawyer's eyes gleamed. 'First, you probably know Daniel made a will, left everything to you?'

Kilgannon felt his scalp prickle, his thoughts again begin to race.

'No. No, I didn't know that.'

'Well, he did, a long time ago – and since then he's become a wealthy man.'

'That's good news, isn't it? So what don't you like?'

'Three weeks ago, Amy walked out on you. Everybody in Straw knows she went to live with your brother, Daniel. Today, your house burnt down. Today, Daniel was murdered. And, as of today, everything he owned in the world is yours. That includes the house.'

'It's not my style, Courtney.'

'Nevertheless, it's now yours.'

'I don't want it, I'll never live in it.' Kilgannon paused, thought, said, 'Who says Daniel was murdered? If memory serves me right, the only person I've talked to is Salty Wood, in confidence.'

'One of the outlying ranchers had a couple of riders out after strays, before dawn. They saw you in the hollow, watched from a distance. You were talking for some time with what they say looked like a pretty wild bunch.' He hesitated. 'You left first, then the others. After a while the two cowboys rode down, found what was left of Daniel Kilgannon.'

'They leave him there?'

Flynn's jaw tightened. 'What d'you take them for, John?'

Kilgannon sighed. 'They cut him down, brought him in?'

'Yes. Then tried to find you, but you'd left town.'

Kilgannon looked up the slope of Main Street, saw the single oil lamp glowing outside the undertakers.

'What's going on, John?' Flynn was frowning, worrying his upper lip with his perfect teeth. 'I saw you ride in with that marshal – Blake, is it? But he rode out this morning with Ring Burgoyne his prisoner, so what the hell happened?' Flynn waited, saw he was going to get no reply, and said, 'Blake looked shaky coming in, but if you were with him then whatever's going on must be legitimate.' He cocked his head, again waited, then made a soft sound of exasperation. 'People are beginning to talk, damage has been done. . . .'

'It's the end of a long day,' Kilgannon said. 'Blake's settled in a room at Conny's, I'll talk to Chad, then go back to the rooming-house and do the same.' He grimaced. 'As you pointed out, my house burned down.'

'Talk to me, John. Give me enough so I can calm the town council when they ask questions—'

'No.' Kilgannon shook his head, moved out into the waxing moonlight. 'They'll come to me, not you, but by then, one way or another, it'll be over.'

'What will be over? What—'

'Goodnight, Courtney.'

And Kilgannon left him.

He felt the lawyer's eyes on his back all the way across the street, heard his footsteps stamping angrily on the plankwalk as, at last, he turned towards his home. Then Kilgannon opened the door of his office and stepped into the warm, tobacco-larded lamplight to meet the accusing gaze of Deputy Chad Reagan.

'The wanderer returns,' Reagan said.

The big deputy was sitting with his feet on Kilgannon's desk, a whiskey bottle and glass by his clenched fist, his dark eyes brooding in a glowering face.

Kilgannon took a deep breath. 'Get your feet off my desk, put that bottle back where it belongs, start acting like a lawman not the town drunk.'

Reagan swore softly, dropped his legs and swung out of the swivel chair, came out from behind the desk to face Kilgannon with hands on hips. 'You have the gall to talk to me like that after what I've been hearing? You got any idea what they're saying about you out there, what Levin's advising the council to do?'

'You spent all day listening to rumours?'

Suddenly, Kilgannon was bone weary. Lips tight he pushed past the big deputy, went out back and quickly washed the dried blood off his face and neck in ice-cold water. He gingerly touched his wounds, winced, looked at himself in the cracked mirror, then went back into the office. He dug a clean glass out of a drawer, splashed whiskey into it and sat down heavily. Under the sardonic gaze of Chad Reagan he gulped down most of the strong spirit, squeezed his eyes shut. When he opened them, the deputy's lips were pursed, his gaze cooler, more pensive.

'What I've been doing all day,' he said, dropping into a chair, 'is telling people calling for your head on a plate to shut their damn mouths until you've had a chance to speak out, defend yourself. Two riders brought Daniel's body in from the hollow, said they'd seen you there. You weren't alone. There's talk of you stringing him up for revenge, and to get your hands on his fortune. I don't believe a word of it. But you rode out lickety split, turn up hours later with Brent Blake and no sign of Burgoyne, and I guess I'd appreciate being let into your confidence so I've got more than hot air to blow back at them the next time I'm tackled.'

'Big speech, Chad,' Kilgannon said.

'Yeah,' Reagan said with a sheepish grin. 'And with that off my chest – just what the hell is going on?'

'Daniel was hanged by a bunch of outlaws who've got an interest in Ring Burgoyne. They took me to see his body. While that was going on, a couple of those same men burned down my house. Daniel was a warning: release Burgoyne, they said, or Amy's next to get her neck stretched.'

Reagan's eyes had narrowed. There was a subtle change in his demeanour, and Kilgannon felt his pulse stutter, then quicken. The deputy said, 'What did you leave town for? What happened with Blake and Burgoyne?'

Kilgannon chose his words carefully. 'There was some gunplay. Blake was grazed by a slug. Burgoyne got away.'

'What were you doing?'

Kilgannon looked Reagan straight in the eye, and again spoke with care. 'I didn't say I was there. I said Burgoyne got away. But what I'm doing right now is praying Ring Burgoyne did get back to his cronies before sundown, because that was my deadline.'

'John,' Chad Reagan said, 'I think you'd better take another stiff jolt of that whiskey.'

Kilgannon felt his blood run cold.

'Why?'

'You remember where you were when the sun went down?'

'Over at Doc Thom's with Blake.'

'Right. While you were there, a feller rode in. He had a message for you.'

'Go on.'

'He said, "Time's up. Tell Kilgannon to go take a look in the hollow".'

And the sudden heavy silence was abruptly shattered as Kilgannon spun in the chair and with a violent sweep of the arm sent the heavy whiskey glass smashing through the window into the street.

CHAPTER EIGHT

The most natural act following Chad Reagan's shocking news would have been for John Kilgannon to
rush from his office, fling himself onto his horse, and
race the two miles to the moon-bathed hollow to
gaze in helpless rage at fresh horrors. But he did not
do that. He felt sick to his stomach, trapped in a dizzy
spiral of despair. There was no need to ride into the
night to resolve a mystery, because the curt message
left for him could have but one meaning: Ring
Burgoyne had not made it back to his cronies, and
Amy Kilgannon had been taken from Daniel's house
to the gnarled oak tree and hanged by the neck.

Finding it impossible to shake off the dread that
was like an immense weight bearing down on his
shoulders, he walked heavily and without conscious
thought up the street to Conny McPolin's rooming-
house, approached the desk in the lamplit hallway
and banged his palm on the brass bell.

When the lovely proprietor emerged from her
room, pale hands fixing the pins holding her dark
hair, the widening of her eyes told him that the shock
he was experiencing was etched deep in the drawn

lines of his face.

Quietly, forcing steadiness into his voice, he said, 'Con, I need to talk to Brent Blake.'

She nodded. 'He'll have remembered; I think he's expecting you.' She hesitated, then said, 'I heard glass breaking, down the street...?'

'Nothing to worry about.' He smiled. 'High-spirited cowboys heading home, something like that . . . if you tell me which room he's in. . . .'

'Up the stairs, number two.' He went to walk past her, and she took hold of his arm. 'John, I heard about Daniel and I'm so sorry. I've heard people talking, too, and it's crazy because I know you had nothing to do with what happened.'

'Thanks, Con,' he said huskily.

'But what does Daniel's death mean for you and Amy?' Her eyes were searching his face. 'Is there any chance, now, that you and she can . . . ?'

He stopped her by gently putting a finger to her lips. 'We'll talk about that another time, Con. Right now I need to see Blake.'

Her hand lingered for an instant on his arm. Then she nodded and stepped away and he clattered up the stairs and located the room with a sliver of yellow light under the door, tapped once, and was let in by the tall man with the bandaged head who immediately sat down on the bed with his back to the wall.

'Kilgannon?'

'Right.'

Blake laughed mirthlessly. 'I should have asked before I let you in. I guess that's what blindness does for you: throws common sense out of the window, makes an experienced lawman act like a greenhorn.'

'You're safe. Anyone coming up here has to get past Conny.'

'Yeah. And who am I kidding, a blind man poses no threat.'

'You heard the doc: your sight'll be back in the blink of an eye,' Kilgannon said, and smiled crookedly as Blake chuckled at his choice of words.

'So?' Blake said.

'What am I here for?' Kilgannon thought for a moment. 'I was holding Ring Burgoyne for the murder of a cowboy. But he got loose, and on the ride back into town you mentioned something about a complex case – and there have been . . . incidents. . . .'

'One way of putting it. Burgoyne's loose. Your brother's dead. Suspicious fingers are pointing your way.'

'You've been busy.'

'It's my job. And Conny's been talking to friends of yours.'

'Salty?'

'And the lawyer, Courtney Flynn.'

Kilgannon nodded, and couldn't help wondering with some trepidation what, and how much, Flynn and the old trapper had said. 'Never mind that, what about Burgoyne? What deep game is he playing?'

'Ring Burgoyne,' Blake said, 'has a reputation as an explosives expert. He rode all the way from Texas to Montana with a bunch of fellers with their sights set on the Missouri Pacific Railroad. Fast guns Arnie Hack, Matt D'Souza, together bossing an assortment of low life ruffians—'

'Four of them,' Kilgannon said, and Blake nodded.

'But Burgoyne, the dynamite kid, is also hot tempered,' he said, 'and, as you know, he went off half cocked, plugged an innocent ranch hand and ended up in one of your cells. Leaving Hack and D'Souza with the manpower to stop a train, but no means of opening a safe.'

'But that makes it easy,' Kilgannon objected. 'Burgoyne's out of jail, they'll be ready to move and you know their plans. In this neck of the woods there's only one place a train can be stopped: maybe five miles north it emerges from a cutting through a downhill grade, comes out with brakes still applied and red hot so it's damn near down to walking pace. We muster a posse, and lie in wait.' He hesitated a moment, thinking, then said, 'There's a deserted shack in an elevated position, set back in the woods but with a clear view. I can't think of a better place to wait.'

'What if the train robbers spot you, back off, melt away into the woods, return on another night.'

'They won't, that shack's part of the scenery – but if that bothers you, you think it won't work, have 'em put extra guards in the train's mail car.'

'Permanently? The railroad can't bear the cost.'

'Then hunt the gang down, drive them out of Montana.'

'This is happening here, you're the town marshal. Can you come up with a dozen men in Straw willing to give up their time, risk their necks?'

'Let's leave that for a minute.' Kilgannon was back-tracking, thinking over what had been said. 'We keep coming back to mention of Montana: you said Burgoyne rode into Montana; I'm suggesting we drive them out of Montana. So it's finally sunk in, got me interested: what the hell is this gang doing in Montana when they could be robbing railroads closer to home?'

'I told you: the Missouri Pacific.'

'That the only railroad in the West?'

'Maybe the only one they ain't hit.'

Kilgannon shook his head. 'I doubt it. I also doubt they came here because they saw a marshal open to . . . persuasion. So what did bring them?'

Blake's tobacco sack was on the table by the bed. Kilgannon took them, rolled two cigarettes. He handed one to the federal man; lit both cigarettes; straddled a straight chair and did some deep thinking as he watched Blake smoke his cigarette with head back and closed eyes. But the answer to his own question wouldn't come, and he moved on.

'It must have been one of them, Hack or D'Souza,' he said, 'who rode into that glade, tried talking, then blasted you out of the saddle.'

'Not too hard to figure out his identity,' Blake said softly without opening his eyes.

'At dawn,' Kilgannon said, suddenly sweating, 'they murdered and used threats to force me to turn him loose. But they'd made a mistake; by the time I got back to town, Burgoyne was in your custody, so meeting their demands was impossible.' He lowered his eyes to the glowing end of the cigarette. 'They hanged my brother, Blake, now I've got reason to believe they've hanged my wife.'

Blake seemed to stop breathing. Then he shook his head slowly, exhaled, and his eyes opened to gaze at nothing.

'Anybody else close to you they can threaten?'

'None.'

'Then if she's gone, they can't touch you – and like I said, you're Marshal of Straw.'

'More than that,' Kilgannon said, 'now I've got scores to settle.'

'They'll know that. Maybe you're the reason they're here, maybe this is the way they want it. They've pushed you to the limit and beyond, and a man riding his pain and grief loses his fine edge, can make mistakes, leave himself vulnerable.'

'Psychology never was one of my finer points,' Kilgannon said, rising from the chair. 'But right now I've got a painful job to do.'

He left Brent Blake smoking contemplatively, went out and closed the door quietly behind him.

His horse was still tied outside his office. He swung into the saddle, rode off as the door swung open to flood the plankwalk with light, and was quickly out of town and heading west across countryside washed to a flat monochrome by the wan light of the moon.

The wind was rising. He rode hard by the ruins of his house, saw an angry red flickering deep in the blackened embers and coughed drily as a plume of fine grey ash was whipped up by the breeze. Then he was riding up the steep slope flanked by tall

Ponderosas and, as the ruins of his home fell behind him, he followed the route he had taken earlier that day when the wind drove the warm summer rain into his face and, all around him, men in shiny slickers jostled close in menacing silence.

But now he was alone, and the true extent of the loneliness and pain those merciless outlaws had inflicted on him hit him like a blow and took his breath away. He rode into the wind with his eyes blurred by unshed tears, his hands clenched tight on the reins so that the big bay turned its head and snorted a soft complaint. And that act, so simple and moving, almost broke Kilgannon.

So it was in some distress that he approached the hollow and, with what strength was left within him, began steeling himself for what was to come.

He rode through the pine trees in blackness, in his despair relishing the distraction of stinging pain as low branches whipped his face, emerged again into the pale moonlight for the big horse to take the steep bank of weeds and brambles in its stride and, at the bottom, stretch easily across the uneven ground to where the battered Concord stood alongside the old live oak.

Somewhere close there was a rustling as a night animal moved away through the long grass. From the roof of the Concord an owl rose heavily to swoop away on slow-beating wings like a white ghost.

But Kilgannon saw none of this. What Kilgannon saw when he braced himself and turned his eyes upwards was the heavy bough, looming dark and brooding against the moonlit skies, drooping high above his head with the short length of rope swinging in the wind and its end neatly severed by the dawn riders who had found the body of Daniel Kilgannon.

But of his wife, Amy Kilgannon, there was no sign.

The moon was waning when John Kilgannon approached his brother's house.

He took his time, rode in with caution. Hack and D'Souza had dragged Daniel from his home and hanged him from a tall oak. For some reason, they were holding Amy hostage. It was possible they were using Daniel's house as a base from which to carry out the train robbery he and Brent had discussed. If so, then there would be at least one sentry out there with an itchy trigger finger.

Sensitive to that real danger, Kilgannon abandoned his horse on the edge of the property, loose-tied it on the fringe of the trees and covered the last hundred yards on foot, laboriously working his way through thick, clinging undergrowth on the house's eastern side. He chose that route deliberately: it brought him out of the woods at the cleared area where Daniel had erected a small corral and, when he reached there, Kilgannon knew instinctively that the house was deserted.

The corral was empty. No droppings steamed in the chill air, no horses stood dozing or snuffling at the scattered feed. Yes, it was possible that the outlaws had tethered their mounts at the front of the property ready for a quick getaway; but that, too, was quickly ruled out when Kilgannon cautiously circled the house and found no sign of horses, or outlaws.

The front door was ajar. Still wary despite the conviction that he was alone, Kilgannon pushed it open with a stiff forefinger, watched it swing wide revealing the shadowy hallway. Nothing moved. The only sounds were those of the night: the soughing of the breeze; faint whisperings in the dark woods; an animal some way off; the sharp snap of a twig.

The house itself was silent. But there was something in the air – an indefinable something that touched a sensitive nerve, told him that either the house was occupied, or those who had been there had only recently left.

He stayed outside for a full five minutes, listening. Then, when nothing stirred, he went inside and searched swiftly but efficiently, sweeping from ground floor to first floor, seeing clear evidence that the outlaws had been there; seeing, too, the more homely signs and scents of Amy's occupation of the spare bedroom.

In the first-floor room Daniel had used for an office he found papers strewn about by a cunning man supremely but foolishly confident in the security of his home. Most were mere jottings on scraps torn from notebooks, but their content was incriminating. There were names, dates, times, specifically named railroad companies – even, Kilgannon discovered, well-thumbed timetables with destinations and arrival times underlined.

He leafed swiftly through the one for the Missouri Pacific, then slipped it in his pocket.

But what deeply shocked John Kilgannon – who

had always harboured suspicions without proof – was the money he found stuffed deep into cupboards in Daniel's bedroom: money in linen sacks stamped with the names of those railroads; stolen money in notes, coin and bonds, a fortune illicitly gained and carelessly tossed aside until needed.

Daniel, Kilgannon realized miserably, had been riding with owlhoots for years. He was a thief, probably a killer, and had been riding the owlhoot trail with Hack and D'Souza – and today those men had pounced on him and strung him up from a tall tree.

Why?

The easy answer, Kilgannon acknowledged as he left the house and made his stumbling way back through the dark woods to his horse, was that Ring Burgoyne was in a jail cell awaiting trial, and they had needed a lever to use on the Marshal of Straw. Daniel was the marshal's brother. Unlike Burgoyne, he was expendable.

Yet, as he climbed into the saddle and pointed the bay's nose towards Straw, Kilgannon reluctantly conceded, with a terrible feeling of impending doom, that his real problems lay buried deep in his past and they would shortly come raging back to haunt him.

CHAPTER NINE

Night had dropped swiftly, and with it had come the chill that drove Amy into her blankets. From the sheltered spot she had chosen beneath the trees – dry leaves rustling as she raked them together with her naked fingers to form a natural, comfortable mattress – she was close enough to the camp-fire to feel gusts of warmth as the fickle wind shifted and the flames danced; close enough to hear most of the conversation between the outlaws as she curled on her side and feigned sleep.

The big blond man, D'Souza, had at last told her bluntly that they had hanged Daniel Kilgannon by the neck until he choked to death; had ridden up alongside her as their horses splashed across the sinister hollow, pointed up at the cut length of rope dangling from the live oak's massive, lightning-scarred bough and grinned fiendishly when he remarked that, hell, they could hang the whole Kilgannon clan from that old oak and still have room to string up a medium-sized posse.

Amy had felt no sadness then, felt none now. Daniel had for some time been but a distant relative, even though he lived just a couple of miles from the home she shared with John Kilgannon. His house had simply been the convenient refuge from which she had planned to look back on her marriage as a dispassionate observer, clinically examining where she had gone wrong, where John had gone wrong. Yet even before a single day had passed she had reached the sorry conclusion that the only time either of them had put a foot out of place was when she moved out, and the next three weeks had been spent wondering how she could possibly find the much greater courage needed to return and face the man she had hurt so badly.

'Shoulda stayed,' one of the men was saying, eerily cutting into her thoughts, and Amy flicked her eyes half open – the right one now almost closed, the flesh around it turning an ugly purple – and saw through the narrow slits that it was Hack, the knife-scarred outlaw with the blind left eye. 'Shoulda stayed in that house until Kilgannon came a-hunting.'

'That ain't the way he wants it,' D'Souza said and, not for the first time, Amy wondered absently about the mysterious 'he' who had from time to time slipped into the outlaws' conversation.

'What he wants,' Hack said, 'is still a doggone mystery to me.'

'He wanted Daniel Kilgannon hanged – that's been done,' D'Souza cut in. 'He wanted the woman taken, he wanted John Kilgannon's house burned to the ground – that's been done. As for the rest of it, all will become clear. Meantime, we set and wait.'

'Coulda waited a mite easier,' Hack persisted, 'in that big house. With the woman. And all them soft beds up there a-waitin'.'

That brought an ugly ripple of mirth from the other men around the camp-fire, and the two reclining against their saddles in the trees close to Amy. She shivered, and again vowed to risk everything in a break for freedom. The horses were not tethered, but clustered together in a makeshift rope *remudadero*. Very soon, the outlaws would take to their blankets. She would be patient for an hour after that, listen for their heavy snores, wait for the moment when the clouds drifted across the face of the moon – then slip away and cut out her own mount.

But where would she go? The shock of hearing that the house she shared with Kilgannon had been burned down was tempered by memories of the smoke she had seen from the window of Daniel's house; she had, she realized now, subconsciously understood its implications while allowing herself to believe the more comfortable option. But with the house gone, John would be sleeping in town, town was some five miles away, and so if she did escape she would be faced with a long ride.

Hack had finished rolling a smoke and now, as he scratched a match alight, the flame illuminated his damaged face. His single eye glinted as he looked across the fire at D'Souza.

'You left that timetable behind in the house – but ain't we gonna need it?'

'There's another in my pocket.'

'Oh, yeah,' Hack said, obviously puzzled. He

shook his head. 'The one you left was the one you used a pencil on. If Kilgannon follows up, he'll find it, read it—'

'And figure out what we're about to do a coupla days from now.'

'But we ain't doin' it,' Hack said. 'Not in a couple of days, we ain't.'

'So Kilgannon gets hold of the wrong end of the stick.'

Hack's cigarette glowed. 'Is that what he wants?'

'He wants that information put where Kilgannon'll find it – and that's been done.'

'He's playin' some crazy game,' Hack said, and spat. 'Hell,' he said, his voice low, 'if he wants Kilgannon dead, I've got a Winchester'll do the trick easy.'

In her warm blankets, Amy tensed, and became utterly still as her ears strained to hear.

'He wants Kilgannon dead, he wants that cash – and if he wants it done his way, then that's the way it'll get done.'

And then, from the woods alongside Amy, one of the outlaws called, 'Rider coming!' and they all heard the thud of hooves, the snapping of twigs as a horse cut across the edge of the trail and burst into the ever-shifting pool of firelight.

CHAPTER TEN

Once again it was sunrise when he rode back into Straw, and now Kilgannon was rocking in the saddle: he had not slept for twenty-four hours, his big bay mare had covered too many miles, and he knew that unless both of them got much-needed rest then they would be found wanting when the call to action came. As, surely, it must.

He made straight for Conny McPolin's rooming-house, tied up outside and walked into the hall like a man with lead in his boots. Her shrewd gaze quickly assessed his condition, and after willingly agreeing to his request to get Joe Dyson's lad over from the livery to look after the bay mare, she chased him upstairs clutching the key to one of the vacant rooms.

He slept until midday.

Bleary-eyed and unshaven, he stumbled down the stairs to a deserted lobby and hallway. Outside, basking in the sunshine but squinting painfully into its glare, he looked down the street towards the jail, absently rubbed his bristly jaw with fingers and thumb while recalling his acrimonious meeting with

Abraham Levin, then turned away and walked up the hill.

Levin was probably still sniffing around, and Kilgannon was in need of good old-fashioned common sense, not scathing comments from the man who'd pinned a badge on his vest and now seemed bent on removing him from office.

At that time of day people were taking a break and there was a pleasant buzz of conversation in the Phoenix. Kilgannon stopped for a moment inside the doors, nodded to a couple of acquaintances as he let the atmosphere envelope him like a warm, familiar blanket. Then, as his eyes again readjusted, he saw Salty Wood calling him over. The grizzled old-timer tossed his towel to an assistant, then came out from behind the bar and led the way into the back room.

It was his living-quarters, a trapper's room filled with animal skins and assorted weapons, an iron stove, and a bunk piled with blankets that might have come straight out of a mountain cabin where a grizzly bear had spent a restless night.

Wood wasted no time. He dragged a couple of chairs out from the rough plank table still bearing his breakfast dishes, both men sat down, and the saloonist fired up a cigarette and began talking.

'You look bushed.'

'I've slept the morning away.'

'Let's hope so. You've got work to do.'

Kilgannon lifted an eyebrow. 'You taking over from Levin?'

Wood spat a shred of tobacco, demonstrating his contempt. 'You rode out yesterday, so did I.' He stud-

ied Kilgannon. 'And you hit trouble, came through it
– but Amy didn't go free?'

'Keep talking.'

Wood flicked ash, waited, let the moment stretch,
then said, 'I've located where those fellers're holdin'
her.'

'Have you, by God!' Kilgannon said softly, his
heartbeat quickening.

'Way I figured it,' Wood said, 'they were lyin' low
at Daniel's place.' He looked at Kilgannon, saw his
nod, went on, 'I followed your trail a ways, then cut
off through the hollow past that old Concord,
followed the defile through the trees and about two
miles beyond that I damn near rode up on a couple
of fellers building a fire beneath a rocky knoll deep
in thick timber. I backed off, went close on foot,
settled down to wait – as it turned out, for most of the
damned day. But it paid off. About three, shadows
lengthening, four more of 'em rode in; from the
direction it looked like they'd cut across country
from Daniel's place, come through the hollow and
rode straight past me. Amy was with them, sporting a
black eye, lookin' pale but defiant.' He let that sink
in, then said, 'They were well settled in when that
feller Burgoyne rode up, and there was a lot of back-
slappin' and joshin' and that's when I backtracked
and got out of there.'

Kilgannon said, 'Two miles to the hollow, a couple
more – so you'd put them some five miles north of
Straw?'

'Within spittin' distance,' Salty Wood said point-
edly, 'of the Missouri Pacific Railroad.'

Wood's apparent knowledge of the planned train robbery took Kilgannon by surprise.

'You been talking to the federal man, Brent Blake?'

'Every man and his dog's been calling in on that feller,' Wood said. 'All I know is rumours were buzzin' like flies round a dead sheep. I had to get things straight in my head so I went over and had a chat.' He squinted at Kilgannon. 'We had it figured wrong. Burgoyne wasn't giving the orders. Those fellers Hack and D'Souza wanted him out of that cell so's he could do a job for them.'

'Opening a safe.' Kilgannon nodded. 'But if Blake was that open about the robbery, he must also have told you how he got shot.'

'He said he'd just finished clearin' up after a rest spell drinkin' hot java when some feller rode up shoutin' about Burgoyne. There was gunplay, Blake got plugged and lost interest for a while. Next thing he knows is you turned up, and the feller shot him must've rode off – takin' Burgoyne with him.'

'Yeah, something like that.'

'Kinda convenient,' Wood said innocently, 'Blake losing his sight.'

'How is he now?'

'Light and shade. Shadows moving against the window.'

'So it's coming back?'

'I'd say so. Which suggests it'd be in your interest to put Ring Burgoyne back behind bars before Blake gets a real good look at you.' Wood stubbed out his cigarette, looked sideways at Kilgannon and said, 'As you'll be seein' Pike about replacin' the six-gun you lost in the fire, you'll have no more use for my old shootin' iron. Not,' he added slyly, 'that you needed it yesterday, the way things worked out.'

'As it happens, a rattler was curled up in long grass, spooked the bay,' Kilgannon said, unbuckling the old-timer's gunbelt and slamming it down on the table. 'I finished him with a single shot.'

'That's the kind of shooting you'll need,' Wood said, his bearded face without expression, 'when you ride out after Burgoyne.'

On leaving the Phoenix, Kilgannon crossed the road to the gunsmith's shop. It had just reopened for the afternoon. Jim Pike was out, but in the heat and the dust drifting in through the open door his son served Kilgannon competently and he left with a new gunbelt strapped around his waist, a gleaming Colt .45 in the holster.

Out on the plankwalk once more, ears assailed by the mid-afternoon clamour, he hesitated, then turned left and walked up the busy street to the undertakers where he arranged Daniel's funeral for later that afternoon. He declined with a barely suppressed shudder when asked if he wished to view the body; memories of Daniel alive were preferable to grisly images of him hanging by the neck from a dark, rain-drenched oak, or lying pale and lifeless in a crude wooden casket.

That done with, and knowing he was tempting fate but determined to keep Blake abreast of events, he walked down the slope to Conny's rooming-house and went straight upstairs to the federal man's room. He was at the window and seemed to be staring down at the street with intense interest when Kilgannon knocked, announced himself and was invited in. For a heart-stopping instant he thought the fate he had tempted was laughing in his face. Then Blake turned and, blind eyes looking nowhere, fumbled his way back to the bed.

'I was wrong,' Kilgannon said without preamble. 'Burgoyne rejoined his colleagues, but they're still holding my wife.'

'Better a captive than dead. I'm pleased for you.'

'Thanks. A man I can trust spent most of yesterday watching their movements. He knows where they are, and the location ties in with your theory.'

'Theory?' Blake nodded. 'Yeah, you could call it that. The robberies they've committed are recorded, we had a fair idea of their next target – but thanks to your watchful friend, this is the first time we've been in a position to do something about it.'

'With Burgoyne, there's now seven of them out there. I've got a Missouri Pacific timetable. Tomorrow's date is underlined, midnight and two in the morning marked with a circle – I'd say some-where between those times is when the train passes through north of Straw.'

'Raise a posse.'

'Or telegraph ahead, warn the train.'

Blake shook his head impatiently. 'You're talking reason, when those fellers aren't reasonable. You put extra guards on the train, Hack and D'Souza'll stop it anyway, and a straightforward robbery – if there is such an animal – will turn into a blood bath.'

'I can see the same thing happening,' Kilgannon said, 'if I ride out with a makeshift posse.'

'Is this a new line of thinking?' Blake said. 'Are you developing newfangled pacifist theories on ways to handle violent lawbreakers?'

'I've seen my brother hanged, had my wife threatened with the same fate,' Kilgannon said wearily, and turned to leave. 'Before that, Amy walked out on me because of the worry and uncertainty of the life I lead. Maybe it's time I looked for a new job.'

'Maybe,' Blake said as a cryptic parting shot, 'you won't have too much choice in the matter,' and Kilgannon pondered on what the federal man meant as he walked downstairs and the short distance along the street to the jail. The answer was to come swiftly, and left him wondering if Blake was gifted with second sight, or had good contacts.

When he pushed open his office door, he walked into a small room crowded with bodies and tension.

CHAPTER ELEVEN

Behind Kilgannon's desk, big Chad Reagan filled most of that side of the room; Abraham Levin's belly bulged towards the other edge of the desk, and his wide hips overflowed the straight wooden chair he was sitting in. Tall, angular gunsmith Jim Pike was standing hip-shot and seemed to be taking up the rest of the available room, his grey head perched on a too-thin neck up in the pall of cigarette and cigar smoke that hung like a thick, noxious cloud.

'Just been in your shop, wondered where you were, Jim,' Kilgannon said, then jerked his head at Reagan.

The deputy glanced quickly at Levin.

'Never mind him,' Kilgannon said roughly, 'get your backside out of there, and keep it out until the unlikely day comes when you're wearing my badge.'

'Easy, John,' Jim Pike said, but Kilgannon brusquely shook off his restraining hand and practically shouldered the deputy out of the way as he moved from behind the desk.

In his seat, Stetson off and planted in front of him, Kilgannon sat back, swung, glared, and finally said,

'So what's all this about?'

'You've been marshal too long, getting too full of yourself; I think you've outlived your usefulness,' Levin said. His eyes were gleaming as he jammed the stub of a fat cigar in the corner of his mouth.

Kilgannon gave a short, barking laugh. 'We've got outlaws holed up five miles out of town, a woman held hostage, plans to stop and rob the next train through – and you're prissily talking politics?'

'How many of those problems are attributable to your incompetence? If the answer is just one, that still means the wisdom of retaining you as marshal becomes at the least questionable, at worst foolhardiness.'

'If that one problem you mention is Burgoyne, you're talking about a man who escaped when not in my custody—'

'With help.'

This was Jim Pike. He'd moved across the room and, cigarette smouldering between thin fingers, was leaning against the wall close to the gun rack.

'Yes, with help,' Kilgannon agreed, guessing where this was leading, wondering again about the federal man's returning sight . . . what else he might have been saying. . . .

'We went over and spoke to Blake,' Levin said, his steely-blue eyes watching Kilgannon through the cigar smoke. 'The stranger who disturbed him while breaking camp was tall, dark-haired, broad-shouldered, lean and mean-looking.'

'And if that sounds uncannily like a description of Marshal John Kilgannon right now, then Blake also reckons the voices ain't too dissimilar.' This was Pike again. His usually friendly face was an unreadable mask. 'He saw the man who rode up and gunned him down. So far, because of his injury, he ain't seen you.'

'But what you told your deputy,' Levin said, 'was those outlaws had you in a squeeze: release Burgoyne, or your wife dies.' He smiled coldly. 'You didn't have Burgoyne, but you knew where he was – and you say your wife's still alive?'

'In my experience,' Kilgannon said, ignoring the accusation implicit in the question, 'tall, dark, mean-looking men with voices roughened by talk, smoke and strong liquor are mighty thick on the ground. If you've got something to say that amounts to more than vague suspicion, spit it out. If not, give your voices a rest—'

'Leaving the Burgoyne affair to one side, Courtney Flynn has reluctantly admitted that you stand to inherit your brother's estate,' Levin cut in bluntly. 'Your wife left you for your brother, he's now dead – and suddenly you're a rich man. There's a lot there that's difficult for honest men to swallow. So I insist that you hand over to Deputy Reagan, let the town see that their councillors are untainted by—'

Kilgannon leaned forward, slammed his fist on the desk.

'Never mind tainted, what about foolhardiness? If retaining me is questionable wisdom, what the hell do you call putting a raw deputy in charge of opera-tions when we've got, at best, some thirty-six hours before outlaws stop a Missouri Pacific train and Ring

Burgoyne blows the safe?'

The silence filled the room.

'How d'you know that?'

Kilgannon shot a glance at Chad Reagan, and lifted a conciliatory hand.

'My apologies for running you down like that. You're a fine deputy. But my brother was involved with Hack and D'Souza – has been for years. I've got railway timetables, indications that the next train through is the target. Today's Tuesday. That train's due between midnight and two Wednesday night, Thursday morning. There's only one place it can be stopped.'

'The cutting,' Reagan said. 'You talked this over with Blake?'

Kilgannon nodded.

Reagan looked at Levin. 'So the federal marshal still trusts Kilgannon. Isn't that good enough for you?'

The councillor strained forward to mash his cigar in the ashtray. 'No. Bad blood will out. Dig deep into your boss's past and you'll come across a gunslinger bearing the name of Kilgannon. Coincidence plays no part in my life. I've been giving Marshal Kilgannon here the benefit of the doubt for a couple of years, but—'

'Christ,' Kilgannon said, 'is that what this is about? All this time, and it's just struck me: you're one of the Louisiana Levins. You think I was mixed up in those killings, more than twenty years back.'

'Never mind what I think—'

'No, you brought it up so now we've got company

79

let's have it out in the open—'

'Gentlemen!' Jim Pike eased away from the wall and dropped his cigarette into the ashtray, his eyes angry. 'I don't know what this is about, don't really care. If Kilgannon's right about those outlaws, we need to move fast. If we have doubts about his capabilities, they must be resolved another time. You, Abraham—'

'Yes, all right, I'll see to it.' The big man brushed Pike away with a wave of the hand. 'Leave us alone,' he said curtly, 'both of you. Reagan, do something useful, take a walk around town. Jim, aren't you needed at the shop?'

Across Levin's huge bulk, Kilgannon watched in stunned silence as a mortified deputy and a very angry town councillor stormed out into the late afternoon sunshine. This is my office, he thought. This is my kingdom, my domain, the badge is still pinned to my vest yet my authority is being usurped by a cunning man no better than Ring Burgoyne. A man in some ways much worse than the outlaw, for while Burgoyne openly plies his trade on the wrong side of the law, Abraham Levin presents an honest face to the world while cheating and robbing the very citizens he serves.

Yet even as those thoughts crossed Kilgannon's mind and, outside on the plankwalk, the two men's footsteps gradually receded into the distance, he saw Levin watching him with a knowing glint in his eyes and knew that, with his job on the line, he was forced to eat dirt. Brent Blake had been right: the decision on whether to look for a different line of work was being taken out of his hands. Salty Wood, too, had spoken with wisdom: it's in your interests, the old-timer had said, to put Ring Burgoyne back behind bars before Blake regained his sight.

Well, so be it. Wood pointed the way, Levin was leaving the latch off the gate by bowing to Jim Pike's judgement.

'Five miles out of town, you say. Whereabouts?'

Abraham Levin pulled another cigar from his fancy vest, the perspiration of strain drying on his face, composure regained.

'Easiest way is through the hollow,' Kilgannon said. 'A couple of miles beyond that there's a rock bluff in thick woods.'

'That's where they're holed up?

Kilgannon nodded. 'It's an easy ride from there to the exit from the cutting where they'll stop the train.'

'To root them out of those woods, you'll need a posse.'

'Even then it won't be a pushover. A few townsfolk with assorted six-guns and rifles up against seven hardened gunslingers.'

'That's your problem. You're marshal, you figure out the best way this should be handled.'

Levin struck a match, stared at Kilgannon through the flame as he lit the cigar; blew smoke deliberately towards the marshal as he shook out the match.

'The Louisiana Levins,' Kilgannon mused aloud. 'Hell, who'd've believed it!' He shook his head. 'They were wrong then, you're wrong now, Levin—'

'And, one way or another,' Levin said, 'you're finished.' He drove the chair back with such a fierce scraping that the flimsy frame groaned, lumbered to his feet, stuck out his barrel chest. 'This is your last hurrah, Kilgannon. Get out there, raise your posse, and hope and pray you meet your end in a blaze of glory. Because if it doesn't come that way then, by God, I'll see to it that you crawl out of here, a disgraced man with nowhere to hide.'

Kilgannon went out and raised his posse, taking his pick of middle-aged men with paunches and eyes looking inward at past glories, youths with innocent wide eyes focused on glories still to come but too wet behind the ears to sense danger.

His choice was limited for two very different reasons. He went out onto the streets at late afternoon when most able-bodied men had headed for home, or for the bright lights of Salty Wood's saloon, but even at that time he would have expected a better response. However, the doubts voiced by both Ebenezer Thom and Levin and Pike came gibbering back to haunt him as he called for help in hunting down the outlaws who planned a robbery and had kidnapped his wife. His requests were met with dark looks from men who shook their heads and turned to melt away into the gathering gloom: from a town marshal trusted and respected by all but a few, he had been reduced to an object of suspicion shunned by the majority; he enlisted a small army, but ragtag at best and, for the daunting task that lay ahead, all but useless.

But before that humiliating experience the Marshal of Straw rode up to Boot Hill in the dust kicked up by a creaking carriage, and there buried his brother as the sun went down behind the hills and the tight knot of mourners bowed their heads and were bathed in pure, golden light.

It seemed that nobody saw the rider leaving town at a fast canter; but even if he had been seen, at that time of day surely nobody would have given him a second thought.

They waited until dusk.

A ragtag posse of eight men mounted on shaggy ponies and sway-backed pintos, with pistols speckled with rust tucked in leather waist-belts, split saddle-boots holding single-shot Civil War Springfields with hammers stiff from lack of use. But as they rode out their heads were held high, for wasn't it they who had volunteered, who had listened to the marshal call for men to hunt down an outlaw band then stepped forward from the reluctant onlookers with hands raised?

So they rode out into the gathering gloom with excitement already quickening pulses, left the yellow oil lamps of town to dwindle behind them as they pushed north towards the hollow and, beyond that, the thick woods in the centre of which the rocky knoll loomed like a mediaeval fortress.

Somewhere in those woods, Kilgannon told them, six men accompanied by an expert on blowing safes were waiting to stop the next Missouri Pacific train. It was due tomorrow night. Tonight, those outlaws would be relaxing – and this was not something they'd learned from Kilgannon (who was more cautious), but something they surmised; something those with memories of Civil War battles like Bull Run or Gettysburg worked out from their own experiences, passed on to the younger posse members, and so encouraged every man there to drink from a deep well of optimism.

Outlaws. Unprepared. The action they anticipated still more than a full day away.

More than that: they had hanged Marshal Kilgannon's brother, and were holding his wife hostage.

Damnit, let's go get 'em!

CHAPTER TWELVE

They rode down into the hollow before the moon rose, harness jingling in the darkness, bright metal reflecting the faint glint of starlight, ahead of them the expanse of uneven ground that would take them past the rotting Concord and the huge live oak and on towards the gap in the encroaching woods that was a natural defile through which they must pass as they pressed northward.

Kilgannon was at the head of the posse. He rode with his thoughts purposely fixed on what lay ahead. Those thoughts had increasingly turned to weighing the advantage of surprise held by a weak posse, against the superior skill and firepower of hard-bitten outlaws led by Hack and Matt D'Souza. He knew that the men he led had ridden out of Straw bursting with pride and confidence but, by the nature of its task, a posse could rapidly erode a man's spirit. Yes, this local hunt for the outlaws was likely to be short and sharp; it was unlikely to degenerate into a grinding, seemingly unending chase across rugged terrain, and spirits should remain high. But Kilgannon understood the vast difference between the abstract anticipation of action at some indeterminate time in the future, and the stomach-churning realization that dangerous, heavily armed desperados were not several safe miles away, but here, now, in the dark woods they were fast approaching.

I'm saddled with middle-aged men, Kilgannon thought, tried but rusty; youngsters thirsting for action but unaware of the realities. Both factions would react in different ways when six-guns blazed in the night, but the shock would leave them all momentarily stunned – and that could prove fatal. Those frailties had been understood and accepted by Kilgannon from the moment he had tried assembling the posse in the town where he was now beginning to be treated like a pariah. He had pressed ahead despite nagging doubts because he had no choice: his wife – departed, yes, but still deeply loved – was the hostage of outlaws; the continuation of his career – to which he was dedicated – depended on his getting Ring Burgoyne back behind bars before Brent Blake regained his sight. Yet even if he succeeded, there were no guarantees. Abraham Levin wanted him out in the cold; federal man Brent Blake would in all probability want him inside a cell.

I'm riding into a situation I cannot win, he thought – and we're moving too fast, and with caution thrown to the winds.

Close to the Concord, lips tight, knowing that to push on recklessly might surrender the slim advantage they held, he reined in the big bay and called the others to a halt.

They gathered around him in a tight circle under the big live oak, horses milling and blowing.

'From here on in,' Kilgannon said, 'we do this slow, we do it quiet.'

'Makes sense,' said Billy Scagg, a veteran of the Indian wars who'd drifted into the role of spokesman and second in command. 'How far to go?'

'According to Salty, about two miles.'

'Then why so cautious?' This was a kid who rode for an outlying ranch. Johnny Kerr, his voice cocky, his pa's six-gun jutting from his skinny hip.

'I know the general feeling is we're riding in on outlaws lying low with their guard down,' Kilgannon said, 'but if you want to come out of this with your skins intact, if you want to see the sun come up tomorrow – you've got to believe the exact opposite. The outlaws are alert. They're waiting for us.'

A couple of the older men moved uneasily in their saddles. Johnny Kerr was silent; to Kilgannon, in the darkness, the young lad's face looked pale.

'Look around you,' Kilgannon said. 'We're more than four miles from town, this is the last of the open ground. Apart from a scattering of stars it's full dark, from here on we're in thick timber – and at the very least there'll be one man with a rifle up there somewhere, watching and listening.'

'Worse'n that,' Scagg said, and he nodded at a place not too far ahead of them, the only way out of the hollow on its northern perimeter. 'That trail cuts through thick woods. If I was an Injun planning an ambush, that's where I'd be.'

'What d'you mean, Indians?' Johnny Kerr said,

then blinked in the gloom as Scagg shot him a withering glance.

'Kilgannon's got it figured – ain't that right, Marshal?'

'You're saying these fellers'll use Indian tactics?'

'I'm sayin' if I was them I wouldn't set and wait for no posse, and I wouldn't fight in the open – would you?'

Kilgannon squinted at Scagg. 'For them to plan an ambush, they'd need to have advance warning.'

'When you were burying your brother,' Scagg said, 'a rider kinda snuck past, headin' this way.' He looked at Kilgannon. 'D'you tell anybody where you where heading?'

'I got the location from Salty. He'd keep it to himself.'

'That ain't what I asked.'

No, Kilgannon thought, it wasn't. Trouble was, the old-timer had hit a raw nerve and started him thinking back over other questions asked, the answers too readily given, and now leading his ragtag army into the woods looked not risky, nor reckless, but downright irresponsible. Hell, with the big man pinning him with his sharp eyes he'd pinpointed the outlaws' location for Abraham Levin, and the councillor had all but spelled it out for him: *get out there and raise a posse*, he'd said – *and hope and pray you go out in a blaze of glory.*

And after Levin had watched him walk out to bury his brother, Kilgannon thought bitterly, he had despatched his rider to the outlaws with the information that would guarantee the unsuspecting posse rode blindly into a hail of bullets.

Well, thanks to Billy Scagg that hadn't happened, but now his posse was gathered around him under the live oak waiting for words of wisdom and he was left with a couple of unsavoury choices: order them to push on into a narrow trail that snaked through thick Ponderosa pines and offered acres of cover to waiting bushwhackers, or turn tail and retrace their route across the hollow with their unprotected backs turned to those outlaws and the high clouds about to slip away from the rising moon.

And, even as that thought crossed Kilgannon's mind, the clouds drifted away and the hollow was flooded with pale light and the shadow of the tree's high gnarled limb lay across them like the sinister shadow of the gallows.

'Turn your horses,' Kilgannon said. 'We're riding back to town.'

But he was too late.

The first shot rang out, its bark transformed by distance into a flat slap of sound. The bullet sliced through the air above the posse as each man wheeled his mount to face back the way they'd come. Most of the horses were caught side-on to the line of fire, offering targets the gunman could not miss. That he did was all down to the panic Kilgannon had predicted would break out when old-timers and raw youngsters came under fire.

The second shot plucked the Stetson from young Johnny Kerr's head. The third wanged off the big oak and screamed away into the night sky. But by then the riders had dug in their spurs and were racing flat out across the hollow, back the way they had come. They scattered as they went, spreading like sparks caught by the wind as each man made for a different path up the steep bank marking the hollow's southern perimeter.

'Push them hard!' Kilgannon yelled, and got an answering wave from Billy Scagg.

Then he let them go. He spun the big bay, reached down to drag his Winchester from its boot and, working the lever hard and fast, sent a rapid volley of shots towards the hidden marksman. He thought he spotted the flash from the answering rifle's muzzle; felt the wind of the bullet that came his way, soft, but too close, too deadly. He was out in the open, exposed, at a severe disadvantage. And now a second rifle joined the first and suddenly the bullets were like a swarm of hornets and he had nowhere to go.

He took one last look after the fleeing posse; thought he saw Billy Scagg on the bank, looking back. Kilgannon gave him a wave. Then he swung the bay, flattened himself along its sleek neck and spurred the big horse across the hollow towards the trail through the trees.

By doing so he was making straight for the outlaws, but giving them a smaller target. He rode recklessly, bent low over the big bay's neck, for the hundred yards that took him almost up to the looming Ponderosas. Then he swung right and rode along the edge of the timber, now shielded by the tall trees and heading east. Within the space of a dozen heartbeats the powerful horse had carried him out of danger. He left the hollow, crashed through the trees on that side, found himself with no easy way of following the posse and instead took a different trail that twisted away from town.

He'd covered half a mile at a ground-eating canter before he looked around him and realized he was once again heading for Daniel's house. The posse was making haste in the opposite direction, leaving him out on his own – and, from their high vantage point, the outlaws could follow his every move as he rode away from them in bright moonlight.

CHAPTER THIRTEEN

Amy Kilgannon had waited the whole of the previous night for the outlaws to leave the camp-fire and crawl into their blankets, but the sudden arrival of Ring Burgoyne had ruined her plans. The man who had come bursting out of the woods and into the clearing where the outlaws were camped had a tale to tell. When that was done, discussions had commenced which dragged on long into the night and, despite her grim determination to escape, Amy had fallen asleep and not woken until the thin sunlight of dawn was shafting through the trees.

From what she had been able to gather from the snatches of conversation she overheard during that long night, John Kilgannon had shot down Federal Marshal Brent Blake after following him and his prisoner from Straw. Knowing Kilgannon's dedication to duty, that seemingly insane lapse didn't make any kind of sense. But when Amy thought back over what had occurred since the early hours of that morning – the unexplained taking and hanging of Daniel Kilgannon, the burning of her home and the way the outlaws continued to hold her captive – then it all began to make a crazy kind of sense.

Clearly, Marshal John Kilgannon had been under enormous pressure to release Burgoyne. The outlaws must have hanged Daniel as an example of what they could do, and told Kilgannon that Amy would die in the same horrible way if he didn't release his prisoner. But by then, for some reason, Burgoyne had already been taken into the federal marshal's custody, and John Kilgannon had been left facing a terrible decision.

If he refused to release his prisoner, his wife would die; if he used violence to snatch Burgoyne from the federal marshal's custody, his career would be in ruins and he would be branded a criminal. Burgoyne's story – and his presence in the clearing – told Amy that despite her walking out on him without any explanation, Kilgannon loved her enough to choose that disastrous course – and she had been moved to tears.

D'Souza had hinted at something dark and sinister in the marshal's past life. If true, then D'Souza's knowledge of shameful secrets would have been pointed at Kilgannon's head like a loaded pistol ready to go off. But to Amy, that was of no concern. Kilgannon loved her still. She must escape. And if, while so doing, she was able to carry to him something, anything of value that would help him clear his name – if that were possible – then that's what she would do.

It was those thoughts that she had taken with her when she slept; those thoughts that had sustained her through the next long, hot day which saw her enduring the filthy remarks and lewd stares of the outlaws as they talked, smoked, passed around a stained jug of whiskey, slept and, for some reason Amy could not fathom, seemed content to wait.

But for what?

The one enlivening note had been the arrival of a strange rider at dusk. The man rode in on a lathered horse, spent five minutes talking to Hack and D'Souza, then rode off in the direction of Straw.

His sudden arrival and departure created barely a ripple. Now, once again it was dark, and still the outlaws lounged around the camp-fire and talked. But now their talk was desultory. They were weary of doing nothing, made sluggish by the heat of the sun and the whiskey they'd soaked up. Tonight, Amy knew, they would sleep, and sleep like the dead. And tonight the clouds were thicker, the periods of clear moonlight fewer – her chances of success, by comparison, so much the brighter.

She heard D'Souza give orders in a low voice. Two of the men collected their rifles and walked away from the firelight into the dark woods. Guards, Amy supposed; then forgot about them as one by one the other men left the fire, stumbled up the slight slope to the fringe of trees where they'd placed saddle and blankets, and smoked one last cigarette before settling for the night. From her own blankets, Amy impatiently watched the red glow of the cigarette ends; saw them wink out one by one like exhausted fireflies; waited still for Hack and D'Souza – deep in talk as the smoke from the dying fire and the cigarillos in their fists curled around their bent heads – to make their way to their blankets so that, at last, she would be the only person left awake.

But when she was alone, still the waiting was not over. They'd consumed whiskey in huge quantities – but she could not risk moving too soon. One or two continued to move restlessly, to toss and turn, for almost an hour. And all the time Amy lay huddled in her blankets and sweated and fumed with impatience.

Once, Hack sat up and looked across at where she lay, and in the brief period of moonlight she saw his dead white eye, the pale scar on his dark face.

But that was the last movement. Suddenly all was still, and the only sounds were the deep breathing of sleeping men, the whisper of insects – the soft settling of the fire and, a short distance away, a gentle snort from one of the horses.

Heart thumping, Amy slid from her blankets, plumped and heaped and curved them so that they looked vaguely like a sleeping person. Carefully, she piled her long blonde hair on top of her head and covered it with her hat. Then she picked up her saddle and slipped like a ghost into the trees.

She waited a full five minutes. Nothing stirred. Stealthily, she moved from tree to tree towards the *remudadero*. Whispering softly and reassuringly to the horses, she untied a section of rope, slipped inside and found her chestnut mare. It was the work of a few moments to lead it out, secure the *remudadero*, saddle the horse.

Then she paused. Despite the chill of the night, her skin was slick with sweat. She wiped her face with her sleeve; swiftly covered the mare's muzzle with her other hand as her movement brought its head around inquisitively.

The long day had not been wasted. She had thought long and hard, backtracking in her thoughts over all she had seen and heard, weighing each morsel of information for its value to John Kilgannon. And out of the clutter she had alighted with considerable excitement on something said by Arnie Hack: 'You left that timetable back in the house.' What timetable? Well, according to Hack it was something they needed, and D'Souza had another one in his pocket.

And that was enough for Amy. Something D'Souza needed – a timetable of some kind – had been left in Daniel's house. Twenty-four hours ago she had made the decision to escape, at noon yesterday she had gathered her thoughts sufficiently to know where she would go when she was free – and now that time had come.

Quietly, her hand up close to the horse's cheek, Amy led it through the woods. The moon stayed behind the clouds; as she skirted the clearing she looked off to the side and saw that the outlaws still slept.

Then she was clear, and out in the open. With a feeling of exhilaration that was dizzying in its intensity, Amy swung into the saddle and pointed the mare in the direction of Daniel Kilgannon's big house.

As she did so, some distance away to her right, the sharp snap of a rifle split the night air. For an instant she thought the shot was intended for her, and her heart was in her mouth. Then, as a second shot followed the first, she remembered the two men who had slipped away into the woods; and, with an immense feeling of relief, she flicked the reins and let the mare run free.

CHAPTER FOURTEEN

Daniel's house was as Kilgannon had left it. He had no key, but the door he had closed was still shut and when he went inside there were no sights, sounds or smells to indicate that the outlaws had returned.

He'd removed the bay's rig, dumped it against the wall of the house, then fed the horse and let it loose in the small corral. But he'd been careful to carry his Winchester and blanket roll with him and, as he moved upstairs in the silent house, he was already planning a night's stay in the big front bedroom which gave him an excellent view and a wide arc of fire.

Sure, his absence would mean the posse bringing Chad Reagan up to date on the happenings in the hollow. But Billy Scagg was more than capable and, sadly, there was little to report other than a hasty retreat beaten by a bunch of ill-prepared men.

That, Kilgannon admitted as he tossed his blankets onto the big bed and crossed to look out of the windows, left him with little credit, unable to offer an explanation, and with Scagg – an honest man – telling things exactly as he saw them. Not a pleasant thought. Kilgannon's one big regret, however, was that by leaving the posse to make its own way home he had no control over what was said to Abraham Levin when they hit town.

He unfastened the rawhide thong, flipped open the blankets, then dug the makings from his pocket. Before rolling the cigarette, he opened a window. Then, standing to one side so he could not be seen but was able to look out over the flat, moon-washed landscape that sloped away in the general direction of the hollow, he smoked pensively in the silence and thought about big Abe Levin and the Levins he'd known down in Louisiana such a long, long time ago.

He'd been a kid, back then, twenty years old and brash enough to think he was the fastest gun in the West. A lot like young Johnny Kerr, he thought ruefully. But Kerr was a stolid, hardworking ranch hand, while Kilgannon at his age had been fast thinking, greased lightning with a Colt .45 and doing his damnedest to build a reputation as a gunfighter.

So he bore a name people recognized and loathed, had a couple of killings he was pleased to claim, a couple more people happily pinned on him without proof but which further boosted his notoriety, and when he joined the posse that day – yes, just the way Johnny Kerr had answered his call to arms – he had been accepted grudgingly as an asset but forced by their undisguised repugnance to ride apart.

The Levins ran cattle on the Red River some miles up from Baton 'Rouge, but the three younger brothers got their cash by robbing banks and had been identified at a Vicksburg, Mississippi holdup the previous month. The local marshal had reports positively placing the trio at the ranch owned by their elder brother. The posse rode in on a sweltering August afternoon when the vanes of the windmill were motionless in the sultry air and smoke from fires racing over a thousand acres of scrub was a white haze across the horizon.

Marshal . . . Tims, Timmings, something like that . . . shouted one warning to the bank robbers, got his answer in a volley of rifle fire that had the posse down in the dust and crawling for cover, and the pattern was set for at least the next couple of hours.

Or it would have been. But, maybe because of the heat and a forgotten pan of hot fat on an iron stove stoked to cherry-red, or maybe because the three brothers set the fire themselves planning to escape in the confusion, things went badly wrong.

The first the posse knew, fingers of flames began shooting through the tin roof of the lean-to kitchen, and the fire quickly took hold and spread to the main house. Timmings – yeah, that *was* his name – told them to get ready for a breakout when the robbers realized they were about to be fried alive, every sweating member of the posse lying in the dust spat and lined his sights on the front door and, when it burst open like a stick of dynamite had exploded in the house, two shots rang out, two bodies were left lying in the front yard and a white-faced kid of sixteen was reaching for the sky.

Only neither of those gunned down was a bank

robber. The posse's mystery gunman had shot the bearded elder brother and his wife as they shepherded their son out of the searing heat of the blaze, and while they were doing that – so, yes, there was a ruse, and it worked – the brothers, the bank robbers, were away out the back of the house and keeping the blazing premises and billowing smoke between them and the posse as they made a clean getaway.

Mystery gunman?

In the front bedroom of Daniel's house, Kilgannon killed the cigarette that had suddenly turned bitter, and gazed bleakly out of the window.

Yeah, Kilgannon, the young gunslinger had held his fire because he was alert, fast thinking, and couldn't see the point in three bank robbers dousing the house in coal oil, setting it alight, then coming out the *front* door, for God's sake! Didn't make sense. And he'd been right.

But the man with an itchy trigger finger never did own up, every man in the posse looked Timmings in the eye, shrugged, swore everything had happened too fast, they'd been caught cold and had no *time* to pull a damn trigger. . . .

Kilgannon merely looked Timmings in the eye, grinned, and offered his unfired rifle up for examination.

Timmings wouldn't take it.

Hell, maybe it was the marshal himself who'd fired the shots.

So he glared at Kilgannon, turned away – and blame had found its usual home.

Another couple of notches on Johnny Kilgannon's

.45, they said, rode in the posse as a sworn-in member all legal like but, Jesus, that kid was just waiting for an excuse. . . .

And that was what the son, Abraham Levin, heard; that was what he believed; and twenty years later their paths crossed again in Straw, Montana.

Kilgannon was down in the kitchen finishing off a meal of cold jerky and dry bread washed down with some of Daniel's fine whiskey – my whiskey, now, Kilgannon thought wonderingly – when he sensed rather than heard someone approaching the house. The glass clattered onto the table, slopping whiskey as he bolted for the door and took the stairs two at a time. He slammed into the front bedroom, grabbed the Winchester from the bed and was levering a shell into the breech as he approached the window.

He couldn't imagine what he had heard, or how he had heard it, for in the distance just a single horse was emerging from the trees on the far side of the moonlit pasture. Its rider held it there, an indistinct figure lost in the deep shadows cast by the moon. Then, brazenly, the rider brought the horse out from cover and commenced to approach the house by the direct route – straight across the open grassland. Of the rider's face, nothing could be seen, but Kilgannon caught the glint of metal at the man's waist and knew the rider was holding pistol or rifle.

One man. But he'd have a partner. That second man would be waiting until his bold *compadre* grabbed Kilgannon's attention, then he'd make his move.

Well, Kilgannon thought, I can't do anything about the man I can't see, so. . . .

The window was still open. A cynical smile tugging at his lips, he poked the rifle muzzle forward, took a sight, and squeezed the trigger.

It was as if the sudden emergence of Abraham Levin as a threat to his very existence had transported John Kilgannon back in time until he had once again become that brash youth hell bent on becoming a gunfighter. In the years since then his character had been modified by circumstances and maturity: the man he was now would never, in cold blood, shoot a man's horse out from under him.

He was still marvelling at the depths to which he had sunk when the horse's knees buckled and it went down in a crumpled heap, flinging its rider headlong. As the man flopped down, his hat spun away as if caught by the wind. His naked head hit the ground hard and, in the thin moonlight, Kilgannon saw a mass of flaxen hair tumble loose – and in his chest his heart froze.

Not a man. A woman.

'Amy,' Kilgannon whispered. 'Oh my God – Amy!' — and then the rifle had fallen from his grip to clatter on the floor as he raced from the room, down the stairs and out the front door, his stride lengthening and his breath catching in his throat like a man in danger of suffocation as he pounded towards the figure lying curled up, and ominously still.

CHAPTER FIFTEEN

'You tellin' me totin' all this stuff was a waste of time and effort?' Ring Burgoyne said.

'What I'm sayin',' D'Souza said, 'is it sets and waits a while.'

'Because Abe Levin says so?'

The man who had gunned down a cowpoke and come close to ruining the planned train robbery by his incarceration in a strap-steel cell was hunkered down alongside his saddle-bags on the edge of the woods. Both bags were unbuckled. Dirty yellow tubes of dynamite had tumbled out onto the thick carpet of pine needles, and the outlaw was carelessly flipping one of them end over end in his big hand as he glowered at D'Souza.

'Levin calls the shots,' D'Souza said.

He was by the camp-fire that had been burning for almost two days, idly poking with a crooked stick at the blackened coffee pot suspended in the flames.

They'd breakfasted soon after dawn. D'Souza had discovered Amy's absence, passed it off with a shrug and a grin and told the others she was gone, but not forgotten: Levin wanted her along for the showdown, and her freedom was going to be shortlived.

Four of the outlaws had flopped back on their blankets, knowing there was another interminable day to pass before they moved into action – but what that action was, they hadn't yet been told.

Arnie Hack, across the fire from D'Souza, was also puzzled. 'Wait a while is right,' he said to D'Souza, 'because we ain't stopping that train until a week from now. But you left behind those timetables that tell Kilgannon different.'

D'Souza grinned. 'Work it out, Arnie.'

Hack sent a stream of tobacco juice hissing into the fire. 'I done that. Like I said, if Levin wants Kilgannon dead, I've got a rifle can do the job. But no, that goddamn druggist gets you fiddlin' around with railway timetables and dates and times all marked in pencil and we set in the woods gettin' eaten alive—'

'He's got his reasons,' D'Souza cut in.

Two of the outlaws were now up on their elbows, yawning and listening. Ring Burgoyne glanced at them, then at D'Souza, and grinned hungrily as he held up the stick of dynamite.

'Levin want me to use this on the marshal?'

'Nope.'

'Then he'd better be damn sure about what he's doin', I tell you, because I saw Kilgannon use his pistol on that federal man and he ain't no slouch!'

Picking up on Burgoyne's point, Hack said, 'Raisin' a whole damn army to kill a man, when it's a simple job for a kid with a pocket knife, is just askin' for trouble.'

'Yeah, but maybe Abe Levin's got a picture settin' there in his evil mind,' D'Souza said carefully, 'of the way he wants Kilgannon to die.'

'And that,' Hack said, 'is tied in with pencil marks scribbled in a timetable and a man thinking a train's gonna be robbed – only it ain't?'

D'Souza wrapped his sleeve around his hand, picked a tin cup out of the hot ashes, wiped it on his pants and poured steaming black coffee.

'Midnight tonight,' he said. 'Round about that time, you'll know exactly what this is all about.' He raised his steaming cup to Hack, and grinned through the drifting smoke. 'More important, so will Kilgannon – and he won't like it one little bit.'

CHAPTER SIXTEEN

It was coffee this time, but even that early in the morning it was laced with Daniel's expensive whiskey. And although the kitchen was warm, Amy Kilgannon sat at the table draped in a thick Indian blanket, and only gradually did the shivering diminish, then cease. The amber necklace was around her neck, placed there by Kilgannon. She had lain in his arms, for most of the night staring into the darkness. Waking nightmares had left her exhausted. She would sleep again when Kilgannon rode out, as he must.

'I almost died,' Kilgannon said softly. 'I lowered the rifle and saw your blonde hair. . . .' He swallowed, again reached for her hand and held it tenderly. 'Then I reached you, bent over you and, my God, your eyes opened – one of them, anyway,' he said, reaching across gently to touch her face bruised by the outlaws, 'and you looked at me and that was the finest. . . .' He paused, rubbed his eyes, shook his head. 'You've had that mare for the six months we were together, loved it from the start, and now it's dead.'

'I walked out on you, and now I'm back,' she said huskily. 'In the circumstances I can forgive you for the death of a horse, but how can you see it in your heart to forgive me for that?'

'In my job there is violence, and I should have realized you couldn't stand it.'

'Poor little innocent girl from the East!' Her laugh was bitter. 'And now I've seen enough violence to last me a lifetime, yet still it's out there and it's men like you who will continue to oppose it, to make Straw a safe place to live.'

'What's happened,' he said, 'would have happened if you had gone, or stayed. Now we put it right.'

'I don't understand what this is all about,' she said, 'but your brother's dead, and those men were discussing another man who wants you dead.' She squeezed his hand. 'Do you know what they mean? Has it got something to do with those papers you found upstairs?'

Last night it had occurred to him, while Amy was recovering, that if there were train timetables left behind by Daniel, why not other incriminating papers. So he had again gone up to the office and searched, and this time he had discovered a bundle of letters. To Daniel. From Abraham Levin. Detailing – Lord, how arrogant the man was! – detailing the proceeds the gang had amassed from named robberies over a five-year-period, and specifying the amount and frequency of the deposits Levin had Daniel make in various banks outside Straw.

'I'm beginning to,' Kilgannon said. 'I know I'm a

target because of hatred come boiling out of the past. But when I ride into town I'll carry with me the evidence against one man that will put a stop to it.'

His words trailed away, and when he let go of her hand and stood up she was watching him closely.

'It's not just the past, is it? How did that man Burgoyne get loose?'

'You've been with Hack and D'Souza, seen Burgoyne ride in to their camp, listened to the tale he had to tell. The federal marshal involved is in town, staying at Conny's place. I suppose you could say he's got my career hanging in the balance without realizing it, and the way he eventually jumps will determine whether I continue as Straw's marshal.' He spread his hands in a gesture of helplessness. 'But while I carry that badge I do my job, and right now that means giving information to honest men who will act on it.' He paused. 'You'll be safe here, Amy.'

'There are enough weapons,' she said with a faint smile, 'to fight an army.'

'The outlaws are not after you, not now. Something that was started by one tortured, twisted man is approaching the climax.' He thought for a moment, then smiled. 'You know this house is now ours?'

Her eyes widened. 'Daniel left a will?'

'In my favour,' Kilgannon said, and now his smile was ironic. 'I don't want the house, couldn't live in it' – he saw her frown, then nod emphatic agreement – 'but by leaving everything to me – and because of the way things worked out, the timing and manner of his death – I'm under suspicion.'

'I can see the logic in that,' she said, 'and again it comes down to a situation made worse by my walking out on you.' She shook her head. 'Go to town, John. They say nothing's ever as bad as we expect; that anticipation always magnifies coming events out of all proportion. . . .'

'And you always did straighten out my thinking,' he said. He bent, kissed her lips, said softly, 'I'll see you later. When I ride back, all this will be over, we'll be together, and I'll still be Marshal of Straw. . . .'

Kilgannon's route into town carried him through several locations where he might have encountered the outlaws, but clearly they were still lying low. He did once again ride past the ruins of his home, but already he was becoming used to his improved status – thanks to Daniel – and so the pain he felt was considerably diminished.

Then he was riding into Straw.

The main street was already bustling, but he saw nobody he knew and his first stop was at Tom Morgan's general store where he belatedly collected the parcel he'd ordered. Belatedly, too, he realized he hadn't shaved or changed his garb for Lord knew how long, and he was rubbing his stubbly jaw and grimacing as he crossed the street to the jail determined to get cleaned up and don fresh clothing.

He pushed open the door, stepped inside his office – and was faced by a cocked six-gun pointing at his belly. Big Chad Reagan was in the swivel chair behind the desk. His face was set.

'Unbuckle your gunbelt, let it fall,' Reagan said.

Kilgannon stood stock still. 'What's this about?'

'Just do it.'

'This your idea?'

A faint sheen of sweat glistened on the big deputy's face.

'I'm under orders, Marshal.'

'Whose?'

Reagan stubbornly shook his head.

'Levin!' Kilgannon said with disgust.

He tossed his bundle onto the desk, saw Reagan flinch, then slowly unbuckled his gunbelt, rolled it and placed it alongside the parcel. That done, he watched with disbelief as the deputy took a deep breath, came around the desk and reached up to the peg for the keys to the cells.

When Reagan turned to face him holding the big, jingling key ring, Kilgannon was shaking his head.

'To lock me up,' he said quietly, 'you'll first have to kill me, Chad.'

The big man's jaw tightened. He had his back to the door leading to the cells, the keys dangling from one hand, the pistol levelled in the other. Kilgannon could almost see his mind working. He'd been well prepared, hadn't anticipated trouble. Now he was faced with a stand-off, and short of pistol-whipping Kilgannon and dragging him bodily into a cell, his options were limited.

'Go get Levin,' Kilgannon said.

'Not with you still loose.'

'Goddammit!' Kilgannon said fiercely, 'the only way for this to be worked out is for me to face Levin, so I'm not budging.' He saw indecision flicker in the deputy's eyes, and said, 'You've got my word I won't hightail, Chad – now go get him.'

Then the big man's eyes hardened.

'One way or another, this mess'll be sorted,' he said. 'When that happens – and if it goes in your favour – you'll never let me forget I stepped once out of line and was foolish enough to take the word of a man suspected of wrongdoing.' A look of stern reproach flickered across his face. 'Hell, I'm abiding by your values, your rules, Marshal. You're an honourable man, and I expect you to do the same.'

Despite the tenseness of the situation, Kilgannon couldn't suppress a thin smile. The big deputy had chosen the one argument to which Kilgannon had no satisfactory reply; without saying a word, he turned and went through to the cell wing and stood waiting in the wide passage.

It was with obvious relief that Reagan followed him, saw him into a cell and slammed and locked the door. Then, rolling his shoulders to ease the tension, he pouched his six-gun and went out with the keys jingling in his big fist.

Moments later, the street door banged shut.

But what, Kilgannon thought, was Levin playing at?

Had he consulted Courtney Flynn about the hanging of Daniel Kilgannon, got the lawyer's opinion that there was enough evidence to implicate John Kilgannon as an accessory and press charges?

Or was he relying on a trumped up charge to confine Kilgannon until the Missouri Pacific had been stopped, the safe blown, the outlaws out of the territory?

No, none of those, Kilgannon thought, wandering across to sit on the hard bunk. Abe Levin was the kid who, twenty years ago, walked out of a burning farm-house and saw his parents gunned down. He believed Kilgannon was the man who pulled the trigger. He was involved with outlaws, had despatched a rider to their camp to warn them of Kilgannon's approach with a makeshift posse. He was desperate for the sweet taste of revenge: he wanted Kilgannon dead, and locking him in a cell put him out of reach.

So, Kilgannon mused, look elsewhere, look—

The distant thumping of approaching footsteps snapped him back to reality. Swiftly, he lay back on the bunk, folded his arms behind his head and was watching with a show of indifference when the inner door opened and Brent Blake came through.

'Levin's gone,' Blake said. 'Left town, not been seen. This has got nothing to do with him.'

'No,' Kilgannon said. 'This has got to do with a man gunning down a federal marshal and allowing his prisoner to escape.'

Chad Reagan had followed Blake into the passage; behind Reagan, Salty Wood had drifted in with the hushed stealth of an Indian scout treading across dry twigs. He'd winked at Kilgannon, then stepped aside to lean against the wall.

The bandages had been removed from Blake's head. The scar left by Kilgannon's bullet had left a straight pink furrow – healthily scabbed over –

through the federal man's dark hair. He was standing close to the bars and his eyes, clear now, were fixed on Kilgannon with some amusement.

'That, yes,' he said, nodding. 'But there's also an accusation by a posse member that the leader told them to ride for home, then went over to the outlaws.'

'You believe it?'

'Accusations about revenge hangings and treachery and murder for gain are buzzing around your head like blowflies around bad meat.' Blake grinned, nodded at Salty. 'I got that tasty image from the old-timer over there.' Then he sobered. 'What I believe is you shot me because you had no choice when I was blazing away at you. You were after Ring Burgoyne because you were faced with an impossible situation and half out of your mind – and I believe everything else is bullshit.'

Kilgannon let his breath go slowly through his nostrils, sat up, swung his legs off the bunk.

'But,' Blake added, 'you got away with that just the once, it's something no other man has done in all the years I've been wearing a badge – and it'll never happen again.' He spoke softly, but behind his eyes there lurked, barely hidden, the hardness that over those years had shaped and honed this man's reputation.

Kilgannon nodded curtly to show he understood, then said, 'What I have to say now is also fact, not bullshit. I've got proof a Straw businessman is involved in a whole series of train robberies committed by Hack and D'Souza. That same businessman

114

has been hard at work discrediting me; for a cold-blooded killing he believes I carried out a long time ago, he wants me dead.'

'No prizes,' Blake said drily, 'for coming up with the man's name.'

'Levin,' Salty Wood said, and if he'd been out in the street he would have spat. 'Always knew the feller was crooked.'

Kilgannon lifted an eyebrow at Blake. 'It was you told Reagan to throw me in a cell?'

'You're as jumpy as water dropped in a red-hot skillet. How else could I get you to stand still long enough to talk?' He glanced across at Reagan, standing moodily by the door. 'The hardest part of it was convincing your fine deputy he should hold a gun on you, and keep quiet about his reasons.'

'He'll make a good marshal,' Kilgannon said, 'when I hand in my badge,' and the big deputy flushed slightly, but visibly relaxed as it sank in that Kilgannon did not hold his conduct against him.

Blake looked surprised.

'Why walk out on the job?' he said. 'The accusations being bandied about are nonsense, I'll testify you shot me in self defence – if it ever becomes necessary – and you'll have one hell of a feather in your cap when we bring in those outlaws. . . .'

He trailed off there, watching Kilgannon as he absorbed what had been said, and now it was Straw's marshal's turn to be taken aback. He hesitated, saw Salty Wood suppressing a grin and knew the old-timer was again in Blake's confidence. Then he reached into his pocket, and stood up to pass through the bars the letters he discovered in Daniel's office.

'These prove that when we take those outlaws we also take the man who's been keeping a low profile while calling the shots for a long, long time.'

'There had to be someone,' Blake said, taking the crumpled envelopes but tucking them in his pocket without a second glance. 'Hack and D'Souza are violent and dangerous, but they'd have trouble planning breakfast.' He squinted at Kilgannon, took in his unshaven face and dishevelled attire and said, 'You've spent a couple of days chasing your own tail – so why's Levin left town in a hurry?'

Kilgannon gestured at Blake's pocket. 'I'd guess he's remembered those letters. He knows I've been to Daniel's house – if you recall, I found railway timetables there?' Blake nodded, and Kilgannon went on, 'I think those were left behind deliberately, because I'm convinced Levin is planning to suck me into a situation where I'll be at his mercy.' He shook his head in wonderment. 'The last time we spoke I asked why the hell the gang rode all the way from Texas to Montana to rob a train. You know, I believe now Levin went to all that trouble to kill two birds with the one stone: make a nice profit from the robbery, yes, but at the same time get his revenge.'

'For what?'

Kilgannon shook his head. 'It's a long story, best left for another time. Right now we've got a man out there who knows his days as a respectable business-man are over – and he's got a train to rob.'

116

'And his plans for you?'

'That,' Kilgannon said, 'is something I've yet to work out.'

CHAPTER SEVENTEEN

Kilgannon's release was a formality: Blake had used his authority to hold him, he now rescinded the order and Reagan stepped forward happily to unlock the cell.

According to Salty Wood, if they were going to discuss the confrontation with the outlaws led by Hack and D'Souza, the best place to do it without what was said leaking out to the wrong ears was in his room back of the Phoenix.

Also according to Salty – who was not only qualified to advise on the movement of hungry bears but also ideally placed to eavesdrop, tactfully, on conversations between cowboys and barroom courtesans, dark-suited town councillors and their colleagues – Jim Pike and Tom Morgan had already been in the saloon for a huddled conversation in low tones that nonetheless did not fool Salty's sharp ears.

'They expressed the opinion,' he said, when he, Kilgannon and Brent Blake were seated around the table in his living quarters, 'that they'd always knowed Levin was up to no good, and never gone along with his obsessive attempts to remove you from office.'

'Comforting talk,' Kilgannon said, 'from spineless sheep blindly following whoever happens to be out front.'

'Use it,' Blake said. 'You need the voice of authority to help restore your reputation.'

'That,' Wood said, 'and an act of incredible heroism.'

'Like single-handedly foiling a train robbery?' Kilgannon said. 'Well, that might not be such a good idea, but we've got dates and times, there's only one location worth a damn so we know where it'll happen. Only thing we're short of is men of the calibre needed to face up to a barrage of hot lead.'

'Cunning can beat brute force,' Blake said. 'Do the unexpected, beat them at their own game. You took out a posse and rode into an ambush, so. . . .'

'It's occurred to me,' Salty Wood said, 'that the cunning could be on the other side.'

Blake frowned, lit a cigarette, settled back in his chair.

'You're talking about the timetables left behind in Daniel's house?'

Salty shrugged. 'When Kilgannon rode into that ambush, could've been because he was going where he wasn't wanted. Where he's wanted is where those timetables point; they were left so's Kilgannon would go to the right place, at the right time.'

For a while there was a heavy silence, as all three men cogitated individually on the problems facing Kilgannon that, in a small town like Straw, would inevitably affect everyone.

Kilgannon could see where Blake's thoughts were leading: he knew that his own mention of the decaying shack tucked in the woods, overlooking the only possible site for a train robbery, had pointed the way. If they rode out of Straw when darkness fell and made good time, they would be settled into commanding positions inside that shack with several hours to spare. And this time there would be no need of a posse. From that vantage point a lone rifleman could hold off a small army, or pick off half-a-dozen unsuspecting bandits before they could rally and launch a counter attack. The only problem, if it *was* a problem . . .

He looked up to see the federal lawman watching him with a thin, sardonic smile.

'Yeah,' Blake said, reading Kilgannon's face and anticipating his objection. 'That shack's almost too good to be true, isn't it? If Levin's intent on sucking you into a trap, why wouldn't he see its possibilities, make use of it? Maybe getting you there has been his aim all along.'

'That bothered me,' Kilgannon said, 'until I saw the advantage it would give us. Beat them at their own game, you said. If they're planning on using that shack and we make sure we're there before them, they'll ride right onto our guns.'

Blake studied the glowing end of his cigarette, frowning.

'We settled down to mull this over, but the arguments have been few because it seems to me we're of one mind: we move fast, put ourselves in the prime location overlooking the only place a train can be stopped – and Hack and D'Souza will come to us.'

'But . . . ?' And now it was Kilgannon watching Blake.

'You're talking ambush,' Blake said. 'You're planning to gun down seven, maybe eight men if Levin rides along, in cold blood – and I don't know if you can do that, or even if it's morally justifiable.'

'Do unto others,' Salty said, his voice contemptuous, his eyes glittering as he glanced towards the old muzzle-loader he'd carried through from behind the bar.

'Or be in a position to do it, but hold off,' Kilgannon said, his eyes still on Blake.

'You mean a couple of warning shots to give 'em a clear picture of what they're up against?'

'They'd hightail so damn fast,' Salty said, grimacing at the federal man's suggestion, 'the dust'd cover Montana, take a week to settle.'

'Then leave it as it stands; we go in with no fixed ideas, let tactics be dictated by circumstances,' Kilgannon said. 'We're in position, they ride in, we watch and wait. Maybe all they're after is the train. Or maybe Levin has got plans for me. Anyhow, we hold fire, see which way they jump.'

'Right now, we know so little I can't see what else we can do,' Blake said, nodding agreement. 'So, one final question: who's this "we" you keep mentioning?'

'You and me.'

'Nah!' Salty's tone was caustic. 'You need a mountain man with hunting skills, and that big smokepole. They hear me snap back that hammer some-where out there in the darkness, it'll scare them half to death.'

'In that shack I need one man alongside me; when the time comes to confront them eyeball to eyeball, I need that man to be empowered with the authority that'll impress owlhoots like Hack and D'Souza.'

'With nothing to lose,' Salty said with scorn, 'Abe Levin will take some impressing.'

'So be it,' John Kilgannon said. 'The way we're working it, somewhere around midnight tonight he'll be confronted with the decision that defines his future. Whichever way he goes it's fine by me – and to hell with the man.'

CHAPTER EIGHTEEN

For the rest of that day, Kilgannon and Brent Blake went their separate ways, after making a firm arrangement to meet in Dyson's livery barn at dusk.

Immediately after their meeting in the back room had broken up, Salty had followed them through carrying his muzzle-loader, propped it against the shelves and made his presence felt behind the bar. All the while he'd been grumbling into his beard about the rejection of his offer to scare the outlaws out of Montana, yet despite his obvious disappointment he'd clapped Kilgannon on the shoulder and wished him good luck as the marshal stepped out into the street.

From a brief chat he had with Doc Ebenezer Thom some time after noon, Kilgannon learnt that Brent Blake's head wound had healed well, his sight was back to normal, but that the federal man had been advised to spend time resting in a darkened room. A subsequent visit to Conny McPolin in her rooming-house told him that Blake was indeed upstairs in his room, with the curtains closed.

It was left for Kilgannon to prepare himself for

their night ride against Levin's outlaw band led by Hack and D'Souza in the best way he could which, for him, meant a clean up and change of clothes, then planting himself behind the desk in the familiar jail office and drinking cup after cup of black coffee while permitting the atmosphere of the place to wash over him. It held memories both good and bad, but its value lay in its ability to transport him from the wide arena inhabited by the citizens of Straw into the enclosed and privileged world where the man wearing the badge was all-powerful.

Yet still there were uncertainties.

Kilgannon was confident that using the shack on the edge of the timber as a fortified vantage point would tilt the odds heavily against the outlaws, allowing him and Blake to watch their every move from cover with their rifles ready to pour down a withering fire. If the outlaws attempted train robbery, or the storming of the shack, they'd die. If they fled the battleground, they would not be safe until they had left Montana far behind.

But Kilgannon could not get out of his mind the nagging fear of what might happen to Amy, alone in Daniel's house. As the hours dragged on he became more and more concerned; in mid-afternoon he was out on the plank walk in two minds whether to ride out to the house, when Chad Reagan rode in and tied up at the hitch rail.

'Going somewhere?'

'Thinking about it,' Kilgannon said. 'What about you?'

Reagan grinned. 'Ain't you forgetting you sent me

to check on those cows with slashed udders?'

'Damn!' Kilgannon let the big man past, then followed him back into the office.

'To get there, you must have passed Daniel's house.'

'*Your* house.'

'Daniel's. I want nothing to do with it.' Kilgannon watched Reagan make the inevitable trip to the coffee pot. 'Did you see any sign of Amy?'

'She's there.' Reagan turned around, cup in one big hand. 'Gave me a cheery wave as I rode by.' He lifted an eyebrow. 'You think she's still in danger?'

'Until we've dealt with those outlaws, what else can I think?'

Reagan nodded, lips pursed. 'You made your minds up yet?'

'Let's say using the shack seems the best option, but we're open to suggestions.'

Reagan shrugged. 'You and Blake – right?' He got Kilgannon's nod, and said, 'Then it's not up to me. I'll mind the store here, if you need me. . . .'

'No, if you've seen Amy there's no need for me to continue worrying myself to death. I'll call in on the way to the shack. After that. . . .' He grinned somewhat wearily. 'Thanks, Chad.'

The big man grinned. 'Hell, anything for an old man heading for retirement.'

And so the day crawled by, and then of a sudden it was evening and the sun's rim sank behind the purple hills and the oil lamps cast their yellow glow over Straw's dusty street and, in the jail office,

Marshal John Kilgannon buckled on his heavy gunbelt and took the shiny Winchester clattering from the rack and went out into the cooling air and crossed the street to the livery barn.

Brent Blake was a tall figure in the shadows, his weapons glinting, metal jingling as he saddled his horse. There was the smell of straw and ordure and coal oil and oiled leather and the thin oil a careful man uses on the pistols and long guns he takes with him into battle. And what these sights and sounds and smells did was place an uneasy churning deep in a man's gut, send his mind spinning along twisting trails leading to nowhere but darkness where everything was uncertain but the presence of death.

The sombre mood had engulfed them both, and they made their final preparations in a silence that was more disturbing to a man than a murderous volley of gunfire. Cinches were tightened, cartons of shells tucked into saddle-bags, buckles secured. Rifles slid slickly into saddle boots. Horses were walked up the runway over which street lamplight leaked, and were pronounced fit. Then, at last, feet found stirrups and both men swung into the saddle and rode out onto the street to clatter out of town – and all still without a word being uttered.

They headed north into a silver moon rising above the tall Ponderosas, and in John Kilgannon's mind anticipation of the coming confrontation with Levin and his band of outlaws was again inextricably linked to thoughts of his wife. Leaving her alone in the house that was now theirs had been a mistake. He had walked out telling her she always straightened out his thinking, when to act so irresponsibly suggested he hadn't a coherent thought in his head. What had he been thinking of? 'You'll be safe here,' he had said, and she had spoken of enough weapons to fight off an army and – without thinking, yes, without thought – he had told her the outlaws were no longer after her. My God! He couldn't know that. He couldn't possibly know the intentions of the warped man who was a survivor of the Louisiana Levins . . . couldn't know, but could all too easily hazard a guess.

'You're muttering, Kilgannon.'

'You see the big house up ahead?'

It was on a grassy rise, clearly visible in the moonlight, and Blake's eyes gleamed as he looked across questioningly.

'We stop there, check on my wife.'

Blake caught on at once.

'The clearing where Hack and D'Souza were camped – which way's that?'

Numbly, Kilgannon pointed to the west.

'And if the shack we're heading for is over that way, then those outlaws would be forced to ride this way, come by this house?'

Without answering, Kilgannon put spurs to the big bay mare and pushed on ahead. He cut through the trees, emerged onto the moonlit grass just as Amy had done in the instant before he shot her horse from under her. Moments later he was swinging down in front of the house. He ran for the gaping front door. With Blake close behind him he charged into the hallway and on into the big living room.

'Amy!'

'She's not here.'

Blake pushed past him. A match scraped. An oil lamp flared and was held aloft.

'She put up a fight,' he said, '– but she's been taken.'

The room was a mess. Furniture had been upended. Pictures had fallen from the walls and lay broken on the floor. Vases were shattered glass. And, just inside the door, the floor was splashed with blood.

'If they did this,' Kilgannon said hoarsely, blanking his mind to horror, 'they're ahead of us and we've lost the advantage.'

'Maybe.'

Blake put down the lamp, touched Kilgannon's arm reassuringly as he went by to look broodingly out of the big window.

'Or maybe they came much earlier to take her back to their camp, knowing you'd be worried, have second thoughts—'

'They didn't know she was here. She'd escaped. They came by chance, seized the opportunity.'

'All right, but we push on anyway,' Blake insisted, and swung away from the window. 'Tactics dictated by circumstances, remember? The taking of your wife and what it means tells us to be extra cautious – and that's all.'

'It tells us,' Kilgannon said tightly, 'they've taken a hostage, and they know that gives them the power to dictate terms.'

'Then if they do that, we listen – but we can't listen unless we get close to them, and we can't do that by wasting time talking.'

Kilgannon laughed. He crossed to the lamp, blew down the glass chimney and extinguished the flame.

'I tell you what else this means,' he said and, in the room now illuminated only by the pale light of the moon, his words sounded hollow, distant. 'It means that holding off is no longer an option, gunning down eight men or eighty is now morally justifiable – and if Hack and D'Souza have harmed a single hair of Amy's head, that's exactly what I'll do.'

CHAPTER NINETEEN

It was with extreme caution that John Kilgannon and Brent Blake rode the few remaining miles north to that rugged place in the moonlit Montana hills where the Missouri Pacific locomotive would pull heavy carriages and box cars out of the steeply graded cutting and so onto the waiting, hidden guns of the outlaws.

They rode with the stealth of Indians, threading their way through the trees fringing the trail so that they could follow it but remain hidden, crossing quickly from one side to the other when the way was blocked by boulders or deep gullies, and always looking for any sign that horses had passed that way: dust or the thin bite of cigarette smoke lingering in the air to sting flared nostrils, warm horse droppings gently steaming, the gleaming green-white of freshly broken branches . . . a stump bearing a shred of torn cloth . . . flat stone glistening with droplets of fresh blood. . . .

And always, too, they were listening keenly for what lay beneath the heavy silence and stillness of the night, and the listening they did was for sounds reaching them from all directions because, despite what had happened to Amy, they had no idea if Levin and his band of outlaws were ahead of them, or coming on them hard and fast from behind.

'Both, possibly,' Kilgannon said once in answer to Blake's question, for it was entirely possible that Hack and D'Souza had sent some men on ahead, then stayed behind to watch Kilgannon's every move from the moment he and Blake rode out of the woods to approach Daniel's house.

'How far?' Blake said at last, and for answer Kilgannon led the way over a high, moss-covered bank and almost to the edge of the trees and there held up his hand in warning.

Blake drew rein alongside.

They were overlooking a long slope covered with coarse grass and dotted with rock outcrops and loose boulders. The tall Ponderosas pressed in on every side of an area of perhaps two or three acres cleared naturally by erosion. On the far, eastern side, directly opposite them, the cutting was an ugly gash in the hillside atop which white rimrock gleamed sharp and cold in the moonlight. From north and south the land sloped steeply down to the course of an ancient, long dried up river. The metal rails of the Missouri Pacific railroad emerged from the cutting to snake from east to west along that dry creek bed, finally to disappear into a second cutting below and to the right of where Kilgannon and Blake stood.

'The shack?'

'There. Set back in the timber.'

Blake followed Kilgannon's pointing finger, eased his horse forward, grunted softly.

'Blends in. Looks like a giant took a bite out of the forest, deep inside it the shack could be a mess of uprooted trees, a vertical rock face covered by years of growth . . . or a cabin once used by your bearded friend.'

Kilgannon chuckled. 'Right. Salty'd feel at home. But either you know it's there, or your eyes pass over it. That makes it ideal for us. Hack and D'Souza don't know the area. Levin . . . ?' Kilgannon shrugged, unsure about the depth of the man's knowledge, prepared to dismiss him as a man with his mind wholly set on revenge.

'And no movement. No sign of life.'

'We got here before them?'

Brent shrugged. 'Maybe. What time is it?'

'Nine, ten, thereabouts.'

'Train's due after midnight?'

'If we take those timetables as a ruse to draw me to Abraham Levin, the train doesn't figure in this.'

'Again, what we do is not settle on any one thing, but keep an open mind.' Blake studied the area for some time, his eyes ranging over the open slopes, the glittering rails, the gash that was the cutting – but always, inevitably, letting his gaze drift back to the shack that was like an ugly, brooding presence set back in a ragged gap in the forest.

'If Levin's bunch are here,' Kilgannon said now, as if talking to himself, 'they'll be watching, and wait-ing.'

'But if you're still fixated on it, somehow we've got

to get from here, to there.' Blake nodded to the shack, then looked questioningly at Kilgannon.

'We go one at a time,' Kilgannon said, after a moment's thought. 'I'll ride first, do exactly as we have been doing—'

'In the timber, seeing but unseen?'

'Yes and no. Under cover, but this time not being too careful. I'll take it slow, follow the trees, make maybe two hundred yards. You keep your eyes skinned. They spot me, they'll maybe think we're both on the move, get careless.'

Blake nodded approval. 'I'll follow you down after a spell; no more than five minutes. If I do see them, I'll be that bit more careful.'

'At least,' Kilgannon said, 'we can be certain they're nowhere near that shack.'

He leaned forward out of the saddle, slapped Blake's proffered gloved hand, then eased the big bay mare off into the trees. He looked back once, saw the federal man easing his mount forward closer to the edge of the tall Ponderosas; then Kilgannon's surefooted bay answered his touch and was dropping steeply downhill, hooves muffled by the carpet of pine needles, Kilgannon leaning sharply back in the saddle as cobwebs trailed like ghostly fingers across his face in the eerie light.

He covered 200 yards in a jolting, teeth-rattling fashion, the mare jinking left and right to avoid the trees, Kilgannon one moment ducking low to avoid trailing branches, the next clinging for dear life to the horn as the mare snorted and slid stiff-legged down almost vertical slopes.

And all the time they stayed close to the edge of the timber, so that between him and any sharp-eyed rifleman who might be watching there was never more than a single line of trees through which, from any distance, he would have been seen as a flickering shape rapidly descending.

On the first piece of level ground, Kilgannon pulled to a breathless halt. Around him the timber whispered with the sounds of his own passing as branches whipped back and became still, the disturbed carpet of needles slid, settled.

Listening hard, his skin prickled as he thought he heard the distant whicker of a horse; looked back uphill, head cocked, knew the sound had not come from that direction . . . waited, scarcely breathing – and heard nothing.

He was still straining his ears to catch again the distant, elusive sound when Brent Blake's horse came slithering down the final slope and the federal man joined him on the level ground where high moon-light put his face in the deep shadow of his hat brim and all that Kilgannon could see was the bright glitter of his eyes.

'Nothing,' Blake said, and now his tone was sceptical. 'Not one damn sound, not a glint of metal, not a flicker of movement.'

'I thought I heard a horse.'

'I told you: not a sound. If they're here, they're blind or deaf or just not looking for you because all they're after is that train—'

'Then why take Amy?'

'Insurance.'

134

'All she gives them is the guarantee I'll come after them.'

'No, what she gives them is the guarantee that if any damn posse comes a-hunting for train robbers it'll be forced to back off.'

'If they were watching, saw me,' Kilgannon mused restlessly, 'Amy would have screamed a warning, no matter what the risk.'

'They'd hold her, cover her mouth.'

'Then there'd be a struggle, hell to pay, we'd hear something, see something.' He looked at Blake, nodded his conviction. 'They're not here. We did what we set out to do, got here before them.'

Blake shrugged. 'And I still say we don't know that, but we've got no option but to ride on down there anyway and if we do stir up a nest of hornets . . .'

But Kilgannon was already moving. He wheeled the bay and, this time moving those few yards back into the woods that gave them more cover, he led the way in a route that took them around the perimeter of the open valley and brought them to the edge of the ragged bite out of the trees where the shack was located.

'Every move we make tells me I'm right,' Kilgannon said, patting the steaming mare, his eyes never still.

'Fifty yards,' Blake said, 'and we're there. Then we set and wait.' He was looking at the cabin with surprise. 'One door, one small window.'

'Could've been designed with us in mind.'

'And rugged. Feller who built it used the heaviest logs he could find.' Blake chuckled. 'This place'll stop artillery, be standing when we're long gone.'

But how long, Kilgannon thought, before one or both of us goes on that final journey? Hours? Minutes? With an effort he banished the energy-sapping thoughts and again set the mare moving. This time there was but a few yards to traverse. They pulled in behind the cabin where tangled under-growth left just enough space to ground-tether the horses. There was no back door. Kilgannon, impa-tient now, slid the Winchester out of its boot and went around the shack.

The moon's light wanly illuminated the front walls. It was but a few yards from the shack to the first slope, and from there the land fell away to the thin glitter of the rails in the dry creek bed. Away to Kilgannon's left as he looked, the cutting from which the train would emerge was in deep shadow.

In the poor light, distant objects quickly became indistinct. But, as far as he could tell, still there was no sign of life.

Behind him, Blake said, 'Only way in is that front door – and there's no way of gettin' there without showing ourselves.'

'Got to be done,' Kilgannon said – and went fast along the wall.

The heavy door, made to open outwards, was ajar. Solid iron brackets were set into the walls on either side. A beam slick with moss lay in thick weeds. Kilgannon put his ear to the gap, listened, then nodded to Blake and hooked his fingers around the edge. His muscles creaked with effort. The door juddered open. He stepped into darkness and mould, the smell of mildew and animals, kicked across a dirt floor littered with paper and skins and rusted tin cans and broken wood that was all that remained of a chair.

Blake was behind him, his breathing hard but even.

'D'you look at that window?'

'Shuttered.'

'Right,' Blake said, 'but to be of any use it can't stay that way.'

Kilgannon was not listening. The door was still half open. He pulled it shut, saw that weak moonlight filtered in through a thousand chinks between the heavy logs. In the half light he cleared space by dragging a plank table across to a bunk heaped with mouldering skins, then used the rifle butt on the shutters. Boards splintered. Rotten leather hinges tore, the remains of one shutter fell outside with a crash. The other shutter he left in place.

'Window that size,' Blake said, 'there's room for just one man with a rifle.'

Kilgannon grunted.

'Happy now?'

'Still thinking about that horse I heard.'

Blake shook his head. 'You think you heard.'

'Could've been them coming up behind us, but . . . I don't know . . . seemed like—'

The federal man grabbed his shoulder.

Both men froze.

From the front of the shack there came a grating, a heavy thump.

'What the hell . . . !'

137

Cursing, Blake ran for the door; hit it hard with the flat of both hands; stepped back a pace, charged with his full weight behind his shoulder.

The door creaked, but didn't budge.

Blake turned away, rubbing his shoulder, his face bleak.

'Goddamn!' Kilgannon breathed. 'Someone's walked right up, set that big beam in place, sealed us inside.'

'You ever come across a door locking from the outside?'

Kilgannon stared. 'Those brackets were new – right?'

'Fixed there by Levin,' Blake said tightly. 'That leaves the window.'

But, even as their eyes met in the thin light and Kilgannon turned towards that one remaining opening, a bullet smashed through the boards of the single shutter and thumped mockingly into the solid back wall.

CHAPTER TWENTY

Fragments of ancient bark pattered on the dirt floor. Outside, a twig snapped loudly, a heavy stone rolled: the man who had come silently to drop the beam into its new iron brackets was leaving confidently and without caution. And yet . . .

Kilgannon, hunkered down with his back to the front wall, again caught Blake's eye.

'You hear what I hear?'

'Liquid. Splashing.' The federal marshal, still by the door, lifted his head and sniffed. 'Coal oil, Kilgannon. They've made us a prison and now they're gonna fry us like slabs of bacon.'

Damn, damn, damn! Mentally, silently, Kilgannon fumed at his lack of foresight. Levin had set a trap – but it was one so obvious the big councillor must have been sitting astride his horse, somewhere out there, watching in disbelief as they rode down from the hills, walked straight into it and let one of his outlaws seal the door.

'Twenty years ago,' Kilgannon said, 'I was in a posse outside a Lousiana farm where a couple of bank robbers were trapped.' Carefully, he removed his Stetson, placed it over the Winchester's muzzle and began to lift it in front of the small window. 'The house,' he continued, 'went up in flames. Levin's parents brought him out the front door. Then someone in that posse shot them both dead.'

He lifted his hat all the way up. Held it there. Waited.

Nothing happened.

Then, above them, and all around, they heard the first crackling of fire. Black smoke began to drift, then billow, outside the open window.

'They thought it was you fired the shots?' Blake said.

'Nobody would step forward, hold up their hand. I was the kid with the reputation.'

'And we're sitting here in a burning building,' Blake said drily, 'and you tell me this was something that slipped your mind – even though you'd figured out Levin was luring you here; there's this lonely shack, you think, hey, why don't I go in there—'

'All right, I *wasn't* thinking.'

'Well, feller, you'd better start thinking in a hurry because otherwise Levin is going to do exactly what he set out to do.'

'Shut up, Blake – or come up with something we can use!'

Kilgannon's mind was racing as he registered the anger on the federal-man's face. He came away from the wall, adrenaline pumping, feeling his skin prickle and the walls already closing in on him as the first waft of hot air came through the window and smoke began to curl under the eaves.

There was no way out through the heavy sod roof. If they tried to climb out of the window, the distant rifle would rip them apart. The door . . . no, that had been tried.

Blake had crossed the floor and dragged the bunk clear to investigate the back wall. But, like all the others, it was of heavy logs and without weakness. He swung away, looked from the door to Kilgannon, and shook his head.

'The best I can do is we go out that window, one by one – or we burn.'

Kilgannon took a deep, desperate breath, spread his hands helplessly, thought of Amy somewhere out there and felt the anger well up within him.

'Blake, if an apology's worth anything—'

Something hit the front wall like a blow from a mighty hammer.

'What the hell,' Blake said, 'was that?'

Then they both heard the reverberating boom of the big rifle.

Kilgannon couldn't stifle a sudden grin. 'I told him not to come, but I know of only one man in Straw fires a cannon from the shoulder. That's got to be Salty Wood,' he said. 'He's opened up with that big buffalo gun and, by the sound of it, he's close – maybe already down the hill and on the edge of the woods looking straight across at this place.'

As he spoke, the big muzzle-loader was answered by a volley of rifle fire. It seemed to be coming from the cutting. Then, seconds later, there was another heavy blow on the wall – and this time the ring of metal.

141

Then came Salty's voice, ringing high and triumphant.

'That one took a bracket, Kilgannon. Beam's wedged in just the one. Next shot'll set you free!'

'Be good if he could do it,' Blake said. 'But with that thing he can't fire fast enough, when he's reloading they'll cut him to pieces.'

The answer was a rapid fusillade of shots, this time from Salty's location, and again Kilgannon grinned.

'Sounds to me like he's packing more than one rifle, the second a fast repeater.'

'No.' Blake shook his head. 'He can't reload and shoot at the same time, so what he's done is bring along your big deputy.'

The shooting intensified. With the outlaws occupied, Kilgannon stepped to one side of the window and risked a look outside. As the fire began to rage, the smoke around the shack had thinned. Through flickering flames he could see down the long slope. Muzzle flashes lit up the mouth of the cutting. The outlaws were staying put, relying on accurate shooting rather than exposing themselves out in the open. If they did that, they knew Kilgannon and Blake would join the fray. From cover, they had enough men to pin down Salty and Reagan, and deal with the two men in the shack if they tried to break out.

Behind him, Blake said, 'We're running out of time.'

And a third heavy shot slammed into the front wall, accompanied by the harsh ring of metal and a heavy thud.

Then Salty again, concern adding power to his

urgent, gravelly cry.

'That's it, the beam's gone, now move yourself, Kilgannon—!'

But his words were abruptly cut off as his big buffalo gun was answered by savage return fire from directly outside the shack. Then the outside walls were peppered with bullets from Reagan's rifle as the deputy turned his gun their way.

'The fire-raiser's joined the fun,' Blake said, 'put your friends in a crossfire. It's time we gave them some help.'

'Those outlaws in the cutting have got the window and door covered,' Kilgannon said. 'We go through either one they'll drill us without even trying.'

'We go now, or we fry,' Blake said, and went for the door.

'Wait!'

A long, mournful wail was carried to them on the night air, and Kilgannon's sudden grin was ferocious.

'The Missouri Pacific's coming down the cutting,' he said, as Blake hesitated. 'It'll drive them into the open, they'll be too busy watching their backs—'

As he spoke, there was an agonized cry outside the shack, and the rifles from both factions went silent.

'Let's go!'

They hit the door and tumbled out of the burning shack together, Blake with his rifle at the ready, Kilgannon with pistol drawn to deal with close range fighting. Flames licked at their clothing. Smoke caught at their throats and burned their eyes as they ran clear of the fire and turned, watering eyes searching for danger.

But the fire-raiser was dead. The motionless body of the outlaw lay in the weeds being scorched by the flames. His clothing was smoking. Alongside him an almost empty can dribbled oil into the earth, and already it had ignited.

Blake dropped to one knee, eyes turning away from the fire and down the slope towards the cutting.

Kilgannon was also looking that way, squinting into the changing light, his vision still affected by the bright flames. Below them, down by the dry creek bed, the big locomotive was just emerging from the cutting, belching smoke and steam, showering sparks, its tilted spot-lantern picking out the glittering twin ribbons of the tracks, All around it the outlaws were scattering, spurring their horses up the slopes on either side.

Except for two of them.

They were fleeing along the cleared ground alongside the tracks, rapidly drawing away from the slow moving locomotive. The lead horse was being ridden hard by a crouching, bulky figure Kilgannon knew must be Abraham Levin. And, in the light from the waning moon and the glare of the locomotive's spot-lantern, on the horse behind him the second figure's corn-coloured hair was unmistakable.

'Amy!' Kilgannon said. 'Levin's got her on a lead rope, taking her out of here.'

Then Salty Wood and Chad Reagan were cantering out of the woods and across towards the blazing shack, both men wearing strained grins, both men leading horses showing the whites of their eyes as they tossed their heads excitedly.

'The fire drove 'em away,' Salty said by way of explanation. 'Caught 'em headin' into the timber.'

'Chad,' Kilgannon said, striding to his big bay mare, 'you stay here with Blake.' He looked across at the federal man, got a nod of approval, and went on, 'The three of you can mop up here' – and now Salty's grin just about split bearded face in two – 'then take those owlhoots still able to ride on into town and lock them up. Me . . .'

'You're going after Levin and Amy,' Chad Reagan said.

Kilgannon nodded, slid his Winchester into the boot and swung into the saddle. 'And there's no fear of his getting away. The man's planning for a show-down – he was hoping to stage it right here, but now that's failed I know *exactly* where he's going.'

CHAPTER
TWENTY-ONE

Abraham Levin was taking Amy back to Daniel's house. Kilgannon was convinced of it because, although he had been shocked at his own stupidity in allowing Levin to lure him into the deserted shack, he knew that experience had left Levin fatally exposed. The man was obsessed with what had happened twenty years ago when he was a young kid watching his parents gunned down outside a burning building, and Kilgannon believed that, for some reason best figured out by a psychologist, Levin's lust for revenge could only be satisfied if it took place in or close to another building.

There were also, Kilgannon remembered, thick wads of bills in the upstairs cupboards. Levin knew they were there, and it had to be that money that had sealed Daniel's fate: he had been hanged to force Kilgannon's hand, but by dying he had left the cash to Abraham Levin.

If Levin could collect . . .

With the crackle of gunfire ringing in his ears as the two lawmen and Salty Wood set about rounding up Hack, D'Souza and the outlaw band, Kilgannon urged the big bay mare up the steep hill through the woods. As he was carried onwards and upwards, he was feeling trepidation and optimism in equal measure: winning through would be hazardous, because Amy was in the hands of a dangerous man who had demonstrated his willingness to commit murder – but in Kilgannon's opinion, that man was making a terrible mistake. In the room Daniel used as an office, Kilgannon had found not only wads of money, but also letters written by Levin. That convinced him Levin had kept any link with outlaws or Daniel, a dark secret, had communicated with him only by mail – and had never visited the house.

If the house was strange to him, then, however small, Kilgannon now had an advantage.

From the mossy bank where he and Blake had but a short while ago looked down on the valley with its dry creek bed and glittering rails, Kilgannon pulled the bay back for a moment. As far as he could tell in the fading moonlight, Blake, the federal lawman, had posted Salty near the burning shack with his big muzzle loader then taken Chad Reagan and launched a two-pronged attack on outlaws now leaderless and confused: there had never been any intention to stop the Missouri Pacific, Levin's use for them on this moonlit night had evaporated when Kilgannon burst from the burning shack – so what were they to do?

Flight was the obvious answer. So why were they lingering, exchanging shots with Blake and his men instead of hightailing? Levin had been calling the shots. Had he revised his plans when Kilgannon slipped out of the trap? He had expected Kilgannon to be alone. When Blake, Reagan and Wood got involved, he'd made a swift, highly visible escape with Amy. He was going for the cash, and using Amy to draw Kilgannon after him. But that effectively split the opposing forces, so what now for Hack and D'Souza?

Feeling considerable apprehension, Kilgannon swung the big horse away and pushed on, riding at a steady canter in a roughly south-westerly direction that would take him to Daniel's house without crossing Levin's path. He wanted it that way. He wanted Levin to arrive there first and be lulled into a false sense of security; he wanted Amy to put behind her the intense excitement of capture, escape and recapture, realize that Kilgannon would be coming for her – and be prepared to back any play he might make.

His own emotions were running high as he drew near to the big house. He was conscious of sniffing the air, half expecting the big man again to use fire as a weapon, this time to force Kilgannon into making a reckless move. The moon was now dropping behind the trees, its faint glimmer seen through the waving branches uncannily like the flicker of distant flames. But it was all an illusion. The trees ahead of Kilgannon thinned; he pushed to the fringe of woodland, looked towards a house untouched by flames but in which oil lights shone in every window, and saw two saddled, lathered horses left to roam free over the sloping grassland.

We're here, Levin was announcing. If you want me, come and get me.

As Kilgannon slipped from the saddle, tied the mare to a tree and again drew his Winchester, he experienced a disconcerting feeling of unreality. He didn't want this, hadn't asked for it. And, in a brief moment of horror, everything that had happened since he was dragged from his bed by Hack and D'Souza flashed through his mind: Daniel's body hanging in the rain; Brent Blake toppling from the saddle, his scalp gashed bloodily; the same man, staring out of Conny's window with sightless eyes; Kilgannon walking into his own office to look into the black muzzle of Chad Reagan's cocked six-gun; the filthy shack where the stink of coal oil and the crackle of flames finally drove home the message that he had been a fool.

Then, pushing aside everything but the need to get the job done, he took a deep breath and went across the open ground in a fast, crouching run.

The front door was wide open.

Kilgannon went in cautiously. Inside the hallway, he propped the Winchester against the wall, drew and cocked his Colt. Then he stopped, slowed his breathing, and listened.

Not a sound could be heard.

'Levin!'

No answer was expected, none came.

Tightening his jaw, Kilgannon set out to search the house, room by room.

He took the upper floor first, bounding swiftly up the stairs before again stopping to listen. His heart was thumping, his breathing harsh. Every movement he made was accompanied by sounds, however faint. Levin would be listening. He would hear Kilgannon's approach. Every door must be opened. Each threshold must be crossed. And the first step that carried him into any one of those rooms might be his last, his life snuffed out in the roar of a six-gun.

Palms sweating, Kilgannon went on with gritted teeth.

The main bedroom was empty. Kilgannon doused the light, searched the next room, again extinguished the oil lamp, went into the office and, after a glance around, walked out leaving it in darkness.

And there was a sudden sick feeling in Kilgannon's stomach as he was hit by the conviction that this house was empty of life.

As he went downstairs he knew the advantage he had thought his was still with Abraham Levin. The man had lit oil lamps in every room, left the curtains drawn back from the wide windows. But had he then walked away from the house? From the black Ponderosa pines, finger curled around the trigger of his rifle, he could be watching Kilgannon walk from room to room. He could choose his moment, smile in triumph as he gently squeezed the trigger.

Downstairs, there was a room on either side of the hallway, a kitchen to the rear. With his mind filled with the image of the gunman watching him from the woods, Kilgannon searched each one, keeping low and well away from the windows. His footsteps echoed hollowly in the kitchen as he went to the back door, quickly looked outside, closed it again. He extinguished the lights in all the downstairs rooms. Then, feeling easier but sweating and frustrated, he returned to the hall and put out that light.

What now? Why had Levin lit the house like a beacon? Amy had been the bait, this should have been the trap. Where was he?

Kilgannon had assumed Levin did not know this house. But how familiar was it to Kilgannon? Was he missing something?

He returned to the kitchen. In the darkness he drank a cup of water and swilled his sticky face and hands. Then for the third time he returned to the hall.

And heard a whisper of sound.

Beneath him.

And, as he remembered that Daniel had once boasted of cellars where he stored a year's grain, he at once recalled the hollow sound of his footsteps in the kitchen. Hollow, because he had walked across the trapdoor set in the floor.

'Jesus Christ!' he whispered.

Treading carefully, he went into the main room

wrecked when Amy was taken, located the still-hot oil lamp, lit it. He held it high, walked through to the kitchen, let the light flood over the trap door that had escaped his notice: hardwood boards, no bolt for security, an inset iron ring. . . .

When he took hold of the ring and pulled, the trapdoor swung up smoothly. A ladder led down to a packed earth floor. In the light from the oil lamp it glistened with damp.

Kilgannon sniffed. Coal oil. Was that what Daniel kept down there in addition to dry goods?

Leaving the trapdoor tipped wide open he went backwards down the ladder, pistol holstered, using one hand to hold the lamp, his exposed back crawling with nerves. Near the bottom he dropped quickly, swung around like a cat as he drew his six-gun; swept the small room with his gaze, saw the drums of coal oil against the mildewed walls, the opening leading to another dark room.

'All right,' he called. 'You've got me down here, Abe, now come out and show yourself.'

From the other room there came the terrifying sound of urgent, muffled mumbling.

'You hear me, Abraham Levin?'

Again that urgent, frantic mumbling, desperate, gagged sounds that made his skin prickle.

'Enough, I'm about to count to ten—'

The crack of the shot was shocking, stunning. It came from above. The lantern's chimney shattered. The flame flared. The lantern clattered to the floor. At once the whole floor burst into flame. Staggering backwards, Kilgannon spun, looked up. He snapped two quick shots at a vague, dark shape in the hatch-way. Then the trapdoor slammed.

Kilgannon was locked in an inferno. The earth floor wasn't damp with seeping water, it had been soaked in coal oil.

Coughing, moving through dancing flames and black smoke, he ran into the other room. Amid stacks of bulging grain sacks, Amy was sitting with her back to a wall. She was bound and gagged, her face and flaxen hair streaked with dirt.

Kilgannon lifted her, untied the gag and slashed the rawhide bonds with his knife. She fell into his arms, her breath hot and wet against his cheek as she whispered his name.

But despite the terrors she had experienced, her voice quickly became cool and calm.

'He emptied a full drum of oil, John. Can we get out?'

'Is that ladder the only way?'

'I know of no other.'

He clenched his teeth. 'Then we go that way – and we will get out!'

But by now the flames covered the other room's floor and were licking at the entrance to the grain store.

Grain!

Feeling a sudden flicker of hope, Kilgannon dragged a heavy sack to the opening leading to the blazing inner room and slashed it with his knife. Grunting with effort, he lifted the sack against his chest. Then he stepped into the blaze and poured a stream of grain into the flames.

Over the stink of the flaming oil, he could smell hot leather, and his pants singeing – but where the grain fell, the smothered flames blackened and died.

Dripping with sweat, he went back for another sack. Amy had caught on quickly. Coughing, gasping with effort, she'd dragged a second to the opening and gone back for another.

Kilgannon slashed, lifted; stepped into the flames and emptied the sack of grain; went back for the third sack, slashed again, lifted, poured, walked another step and emptied the sack then flung it down flat like a blanket – and in the crackling and spitting of super-heated grain he saw that he had created a pathway.

'Enough! Let's go!'

She dashed past him, choking, and he held her back.

'Levin . . . dropped the . . . trapdoor. There's no lock, but . . .'

The flames had been driven back. The only light came from the hungry flickering of those around the edges of the dumped grain. In that smoky light Kilgannon sucked in a lungful of air, coughed, then climbed the ladder. At the top he bent his head, put his back to the trapdoor and pushed. He couldn't move it.

Clouds of smoke billowed around him. At the foot of the ladder, Amy was coughing and squinting up anxiously through streaming eyes.

And already the flames, fuelled by Levin's spilled coal oil, were winning the battle against the smothering grain and creeping towards the ladder.

Kilgannon counted silently to three, braced his legs and shoulders, and pushed.

The rung he was standing on broke with a splintering crack. He dropped down eighteen inches.

'John, quickly!' Amy said, her cry of panic coming in a terrible, straining wheeze.

If he went lower, his shoulders wouldn't reach the trapdoor. A rung higher, and his position would be impossibly cramped.

But there was no other way.

Kilgannon reached high, stepped over the broken rung. Knees bent, bent at the waist, head dropped and shoulders hunched, he placed his back against the trapdoor and pushed upwards.

It lifted!

As his muscles creaked, as the pounding of his heart built up the pressure inside his head until he felt it would burst, the trapdoor opened wider and, on its upper surface, something heavy slid.

And then it went all the way. Cool air washed over his face. He sucked in air, called down to Amy, and felt her hand touch his leg, clutch, and with her clinging to him they climbed the last few feet and emerged into the kitchen.

They were just in time.

As they stepped away from the trapdoor and saw Abraham Levin's lifeless body – he had taken Kilgannon's two bullets in the face and fallen on the trapdoor as it slammed shut – the flames were sucked up by the oxygen and came roaring out of the cellar.

At once the ceiling above them blackened, shrivelled, then burst into flame. Kilgannon grabbed Amy's hand. Together they ran for the front door, burst out into the darkness of a now moonless night, then ran clear of the house to collapse, gasping, on the grass.

They were like that when Blake, Reagan and Salty Wood rode up: wrapped in each other's arms, watching the monument to Daniel Kilgannon's wickedness burn rapidly down to a pile of ashes that, in the end, would be no more impressive than the ruins of his brother's humble dwelling.

'We all start equal, finish equal,' Kilgannon said quietly as he stood up and helped Amy to her feet. 'What happened, Blake?'

'It's like you just said,' Blake said, his hands folded on the horn. 'With Levin gone, Hack and D'Souza took off with their *compadres*, but they couldn't stop us taking Burgoyne and that makes you and me equal, back where we started. I've got my prisoner, you're still Marshal of Straw with your reputation intact.'

Salty Wood was grinning. Further back, Chad Reagan was also looking highly pleased while keeping an eye on the horse carrying a bloodstained and glowering Ring Burgoyne.

'So,' Blake said, 'if you've got no objections, Marshal, I'll take Burgoyne and get the hell out of here.'

'And why,' Kilgannon said innocently, 'would I object?'

'God only knows,' Blake said, 'but after what I've

156

seen the last couple of days it could happen, and I don't intend waitin' around until it does.'

And with a flick of the reins he took the lead rope from Chad Reagan, flashed a grin at John Kilgannon, and rode off into the darkness.